To Kacy

Thanks for

brying th

buck you

no-shaw crazy

BITCH

See You Soon

A very special thanks goes out to Liz Cortes for the fantastic cover art. Your design brings the book to a whole new level. I look forward to working with you again.

A very special thanks also goes out to Ryan Abbott. His hard work and dedication to ensure my stories became published is greatly appreciated. He worked tirelessly and nonstop to have this book released. I am very proud to be a part of the RAYOR Publishing family. Check out some other titles from RAYOR. You will not be disappointed.

And lastly, to you dear reader. Thank you for taking the time to purchase and read my book. This 'frenetic mind' hopes you enjoy all 5 Tales of Terror.

Until we meet again...IN YOUR NIGHTMARES!!!!!

RAYOR Publishing

ISBN-13: 978-1-946577-10-8
ISBN-10: 1-946577-10-3

CONFESSIONS OF A FRENETIC MIND

5 Tales of Blood Curdling Terror

Rich Cyr

CONTENTS

ROBBIE'S REVENGE

The U-Haul truck took a sharp left turn onto a small side road. It continued driving slowly through the residential neighborhood. The passenger, 55-year-old Mike Robertson, said to the driver, "Stop right here at this blue house. This is where I live."

Without saying a word, the driver does as instructed. Mike steps out of the truck, his short, curly brown hair blowing in the cool spring breeze. A woman's head appears in the open window. She smiles and says, "Good afternoon honey. I hope you had a great day."

"Thanks, sweetheart. It just got much better," Mike shot back with a huge smile on his face.

The woman in the window is his wife Carol. She is 49 years old, with long, flowing blonde hair. She is tall and thin with curves in all the right places. Mike and Carol began as high school sweethearts. He was the Captain of the football team, and she was Head Cheerleader. One date to the movies 37 years ago, and they haven't looked back since. She became pregnant several years later. Mike did what he knew was the only right thing to do; marry the only love of his life. Their one and only child, Will, was a happy 25-year-old. 5'9", short brown hair, just like his father. He wasn't exactly skinny, but remained fit from all of the physical activities that he enjoyed, such as hiking, biking, kayaking, and basketball.

1

The Robertson's were the epitome of 'The Perfect Family'. Mike had a great career at Lexmark as a Systems Analyst. That was only a title they gave him in order to pay him more money. He began working at Lexmark straight out of college. He worked his way up the Corporate Ladder, mastering every division they had. He was offered management several times, but always turned it down. He loved his life just the way it was, and refused to be stuck working 70-80 hours per week, missing important family time. Mike had seen many of his friends concentrate solely on the money, disregarding their families in the meantime.

Carol on the other hand, had quit working once she became pregnant with Will. She offered to go back to work, even part time, just to help out, but Mike wouldn't have any of that. He wanted her to be able to give Will the best possible life he could have.

The best life is exactly what Will did have. When he was young, being an only child definitely had its perks. He was spoiled in a way that didn't make him selfish, but more in a way that made him feel extremely loved. Many of their friends and neighbors joked that they were straight out of a television sitcom. The parents' names were Mike and Carol for Chrissakes! They were nice, friendly, and above all, adorably corny.

Will was on a summer break from Fordham University. His parents didn't force him to get a job. They valued the importance of a good education. They were well off financially, and loved having Will living at home until he became the high-priced attorney he was working on becoming.

2

The U-Haul driver opened up the back of the truck, grabbed his hand truck, and loaded four big boxes onto it. Mike stood at the back and said, "Bring them to the edge, and hand them to me. I'll take them down for you."

"Thank you, sir", said the driver.

"Sir? No need to be so formal. The name is Mike."

"Thank you, Mike."

Will came walking up the street, bouncing a basketball.

"Hi dad."

"Hi son. How did my All-Star forward do?"

"Come on dad. How do you think I did? I killed it!" Will said in mock arrogance.

"But of course, you did," shot back Mike.

"Hey, can I help you with that?" asked Will in reference to the boxes on the truck.

"Thanks anyway. But as you can see, I have it all under control."

"What's in the boxes anyway?"

"I could tell you, but then I would have to kill you!" Mike said jokingly.

"With lines like that, you are already killing me; slowly and painfully," said Will.

Mike smiled.

"Actually, it's called a robot. Lexmark has a new product that they would like me to program. They are letting me work from home, seeing that I have constructed the entire downstairs into my personal workplace."

Robot?" asked Will.

He began walking in a robotic way, his arms and legs moving up and down in a slow, forward motion.

"Danger Will Robinson. Danger!"

"Dear boy!" said Mike, doing his best Dr. Smith impression.

Is that the first thing you think of when I say robot. The last time 'Lost in Space aired an original episode was 1968."

"Come on dad. What else can I think of. You named me after Billy Mumy's character. I'm sure if you had your way, you would legally change my last name from Robertson to Robinson."

"Who says that I didn't do that already?"

"Hey, I'm just grateful that your favorite show wasn't 'Space 1999'. That show sucked!"

"Come on," said Mike. "Martin Landau is an iconic genius!"

"Yeah, that may be true, but his agent must have been dropped on his head one too many times as a child to think that 'Space 1999' would be great for his career."

The driver let out a sigh as he stood waiting at the edge of the truck, waiting for the 'witty banter' to end.

Will felt a buzz emanating from his back pocket. He took out his cellphone. A big smile came across his face as he read the name Lisa on his phone. Lisa was a gorgeous 24-year-old woman he met at Fordham. She was tall, thin, with long, straight black hair. They were the perfect couple. She loved his corny jokes, and his constant pop culture references to the 1960's and 1970's. She didn't always get them all, but always smiled like she did.

"Sorry dad. I would love to help, but I have to go." Will hit the answer button on his cell and bellowed a cheesy Big Bopper,"WELL,HELLLOOO BAAAABY!"

Mike watched Will saunter into the house. He looked up at the driver and said,

"Ahhh, yes. Now let's get to work!"

3

Carol opened the garage door.

"Hey, guys. Put the boxes in here. We'll get them to the office later."

Later that evening, Mike had all of the boxes opened, and the four printers, aka robots, set up. Each printer had an 'arm' attached to the printer, where a needle was inserted into the end. This was used to create portraits. It reminded Mike of the overhead printers that the schools used back in the 70's. He remembered putting the sheet on the printer, and it would be projected onto the wall. Similar in look, this robot was definitely much more high-tech.

Mike proudly looked at his new 'toy' and said, "I shall name this robot 'Robbie', after my favorite show, 'Lost In Space'. Now, let's see what 'Robbie is capable of."

Mike plugged the machine in, and hit the ON switch for the first machine. It started humming, as it began to warm up.

"Almost forgot the paper," he said, as he grabbed a stack and placed it directly under the arm. Just as he moved his hand, the arm came down rapidly, hitting the paper with a loud THUMP. Confused for a second, Mike realized that he forgot to insert the ink cartridge. He grabbed one from the table, and placed it in the back of the machine.

"Let's try this one more time."

Mike hit the Activate switch once again. The arm raised up, and this time gently hit the paper. It began drawing a portrait of a man. Mike stood there mesmerized as 'Robbie' continued drawing a portrait of a white male with short brown hair. The arm came up once again, shifted colors, coming down, this time coloring the eyes. They were a greenish-brown, just like his. Adding additional features, Mike suddenly realized that 'Robbie' was creating a portrait of himself. It began drawing a huge cheesy grin. Mike couldn't understand why, but it suddenly felt like thousands of endorphins were instantly released into his blood stream. He was always a happy person, but the second that the grin appeared, he felt completely overjoyed. He couldn't stop smiling. The machine stopped printing. Mike grabbed his portrait, looking at it proudly.

"I have to hand it to you, Robbie. You do good work. Now to set up the other 3."

The second machine began drawing a portrait of Mike as well. This time 'Robbie' had Mike looking very solemn. At that exact moment, his mood drastically changed. He no longer felt ecstatic. He abruptly felt very serious, with no interest in joking around, or even going upstairs to engage in conversation with his family.

"What the hell is happening?" he asked out loud to himself.

A part of him knew that he needed to contact Lexmark immediately, to find out what the hell this machine is, and where the hell did it come from. He decided to do that at a later time. For some inexplicable reason, he had a sudden urge, more like a need, to set up the final two arms of 'Robbie'. Again, they were portraits of himself, each with a distinct emotion. One was melancholy, and the other was a look of utter sadness. It even added the special touch of one tear streaming down the left side of his face. It reminded him of the 1970's commercial of the Indian looking at all of the trash. Normally, an old 70's reference would make him chuckle, but all he felt was complete sadness, bordering on depression. Unable to comprehend what was causing these extreme changes in emotions, Mike once again said to himself, "What the hell is happening?"

4

Carol opened the upstairs door to their 3 bedroom, 2 bathroom Colonial house, and yelled downstairs, "Come on honey. Dinner is ready."

Mike shut off all four machines, and turned off the light in his office. Suddenly, he felt very drained, but the depression slowly dissipated.

"That was some freaky shit!" Mike said as he closed the door, and walked upstairs to his happy family life.

5

Carol and Will were already sitting at the kitchen table when Mike walked upstairs. Without a word, he sat down and began grabbing the mashed potatoes, green beans, and a slice of medium rare steak that had already been prepared in the middle of the table.

He took his first bite when Will said, "Dad, what's wrong? You look like John Hurt in the movie 'Alien' right before the chest buster came bursting out of his chest!"

Quoting a line from the classic movie, Will said," Come on. The food's not that bad!"

Normally, Mike would have a witty comeback. He loved trading movie lines with his son. This time he took a napkin, began wiping the sweat from his forehead, and said sternly, "Just eat your meal. I don't have time for this."

Will and Carol sat there, silently stunned. In all of the years that Mike and Carol were married, she rarely saw Mike snap. It was usually the exact opposite. She wanted him to show some kind of emotion. He always responded with, "I don't like confrontation" or "It's not worth it."

Now he was snapping at his family over something insignificant.

Carol asked," Hey, honey. Are you alright? You look tired."

That snapped him back to reality. "Sorry. It's been a long week at work, and they just threw this project downstairs at me at the very last minute."

Carol, showing empathy, walked to his side of the table and gave him a kiss on the cheek, along with a hug.

"Don't worry about it. We'll get through it together. We always do."

At this, Mike jumped out of his chair, grabbed his food, and said, "I'm going to take this downstairs with me. I've made some major breakthroughs, and I would hate to stop."

Both Will and Carol sat at the table looking perplexed, but didn't say a word. Mike knew what he was saying, and to himself asked what this sudden compulsion to go downstairs; his need to get back to 'Robbie'. He opened the door leading to the office, walked swiftly to the office, leaving the door wide open. Carol followed him, watching him walk. When he opened the door to his office and entered, Carol closed the door, looked at Will and said, "Well, at least we won't let this food go to waste."

6

Downstairs in the office, Mike placed his plate of food to the side, and walked over to 'Robbie's' 4 arms. He heard a humming sound, which he knew was an indication that the machine was turned on. Walking by each arm confirmed that.

"That's strange. I'm positive that I turned each machine off before going upstairs."

Suddenly, and without warning, he felt his face becoming redder as intense anger coursed through his body. He saw that Arm # 2 had printed a portrait. He picked it up, and looked at it. Again, it was a portrait of himself; this time with a reddened face, sweat dripping from his brow, complete with an angry snarl. He immediately ripped the portrait in half.

"What the fuck is going on?"

This sudden outburst would shock anyone that knew Mike Robertson. He rarely swore. He thought it was a sign of ignorance, signaling a lack of education. He backed up, hitting the dinner dish that he had placed on the table. It came crashing to the floor, dumping mashed potatoes, green beans and steak all over. Mike picked up the plate, throwing it against the wall in a fit of anger.

Upstairs, Carol and Will could hear the low rumbles of Mike swearing, and the scuffle of the plate hitting the wall.

Will looked at his mom, showing concern. "What is happening to dad? In the 25 years that I have been on this earth, I have never seen such mood swings."

It's been much longer for me," answered Carol. "Let me go check on him."

Carol opened the door, and yelled downstairs, "Hey honey, is everything alright?"

No answer. She began walking down the stairs. She was halfway down when she heard the office door slam shut. Feeling concern, now mixed with a hint of anger, she quickened her pace, reached the bottom, and turned the door knob to the office. It was locked.

"Mike. Answer me. What's wrong?"

Still no answer. She began banging on the door.

"Come on Mike. Let me in. I told you that we can work through any problem together."

That was followed by several seconds of silence. It seemed like an eternity to Carol. Suddenly, the radio turned on, and Mike yelled over the loud music, "Leave me alone. I'll be upstairs later."

Carol persisted. "Please let me in."

"I told you that I am busy. What part of that don't you understand?" was his answer, as the volume on the radio went up even higher.

7

The LED on the alarm clock read 3:07am as Mike
crawled into bed next to Carol. She grabbed a
Kleenex from the nightstand to wipe her moist eyes
from all of the crying she had been doing all night.
Mike rolled over onto his left side, facing opposite
Carol. She put her arm around him.

"Get your stinking hands off of me," Mike bellowed.
Carol, attempting to lighten the mood, and knowing
his love of classic movie lines, finished his thought
with, "You damn dirty ape!"

She gave a nervous laugh. Mike didn't laugh. He
proceeded to push Carol's arm off of him, pull the
covers over his body, and closed his eyes. Carol,
giving up, turned to her other side, and silently
sobbed herself to sleep.

8

The family saw less and less of Mike the next several weeks, turning into months. He would stay downstairs all day, doing God knows what. His breaks for lunch and dinner became less frequent. At first, he would come upstairs to bed, mainly in the wee hours of the morning. His wife's pleas to talk were completely ignored. Will eventually gave up his attempts to get through to his father. He would come home from his girlfriend's house, or from playing basketball with his friends, to once again find his father downstairs, playing with his new best friend, 'Robbie'. Once he tried to sneak downstairs and open the door. The door was locked, with the radio blasting at maximum volume. His next attempt to catch a glimpse of what could possibly going on downstairs, was met with a large white sign that read in Bold Black letters KEEP OUT. Just like his mother several weeks earlier, he gave up trying to get through to his father. In a desperate attempt, Carol called Mike's work number at Lexmark. She let the phone ring 10 times before hanging up and trying again. This time she let it ring 15 times with no answer before hanging up. Thinking that perhaps she had the wrong number, Carol dialed information. They gave her the same number. She was dumbfounded, and felt lost. Will was always out with his friends or girlfriend. She had given up all of her friends to be the dutiful wife. She felt depressed and

alone. She began letting the housecleaning go. She now spent most of her days sitting in front of the television set like a zombie, tuning everything out. One beautiful July day, when she should be enjoying the clear skies, and the 85-degree heat, she opted to spend it depressed, all alone in front of the boob tube. A commercial came on for one of those ambulance chasing lawyers. The voiceover began, "If you have Mesothelioma, call 1-800...... "
Disgusted, she grabbed the remote to turn down the volume, and got up from the couch to get a drink of water. She heard a loud BANG coming from downstairs. She wasn't quite sure what it was, but was afraid to admit to herself what it might be. She knew Mike had a small 38 handgun that he kept for 'safety'. Her arguments about the dangers of having a gun in the house went unheeded. Carol had given up long ago, knowing it was an argument that she would never win. She grabbed her cellphone, and ran downstairs. Of course, the door was locked. She banged and banged on the door screaming, "Mike! Mike!"

9

Not getting any response, she began kicking the door. Surprisingly, on her 5th kick, the door opened. She found Mike slumped over in his chair, with his head resting on the desk. The bottom dresser drawer where he kept his gun was open. Blood was pouring from a huge hole in his left temple. It was seeping onto his desk, which was littered with portraits of Mike. It took several seconds for the shock to wear off to realize what had happened. It appeared that Mike had taken his own life, using his gun to put a bullet in his head. But where was the gun? Shouldn't the gun have done more damage. Sure, there was a decent sized hole in his temple, but wouldn't the bullet exit the other side?

As these thoughts began racing through Carol's head, all four machines instantly turned off on their own. This snapped Carol back to reality.

 Sobbing, she grabbed Mike and began cradling him in her arms, screaming," NO! WHY?"

This went on for several minutes, before she composed herself enough to call the police. She was still in such a state of shock, that her blood-soaked shirt, covered with small pieces of brain, didn't even phase her. The police showed up with an ambulance 5 minutes later. The body was taken away.

10

Initially, the death was ruled a suicide, but the police had the same questions that Carol had. It appeared to be a gunshot wound, but where was the bullet? What would cause him to end his own life? The police coded it as inconclusive until an autopsy could be performed.

11

It took several months of severe depression over the death of Mike for Carol and Will to reach some sense of normalcy. They both knew that they would never be the same, and that they would never fully recover from the loss. If it wasn't for the strong support system of Carol's parents, and Will's girlfriend Lisa, going above and beyond to be there for the grief-stricken family. Even Mike's parents would come over, or call occasionally to ensure that Carol and Will were alright.

12

Once the downstairs office was no longer labeled a crime scene, and the yellow tape was removed, Carol had been wanting Lexmark to pick up the four robots that had been dubbed 'Robbie'. She attempted once again to call Lexmark. She received the same response of continuous rings with no answer. She thought back, and was surprised that in all of the years Mike worked at Lexmark, she never had to call him. He always stressed that she should call ONLY in a case of an emergencies and in all of their blissful years together, Mike never gave her a reason to call. He was strictly a wake-up, go to work, come home straight from work, enjoy some family time, go to bed, wake-up, and start this process all over again. In those rare occasions that he would be late, he would call her. She went through her phone to see if she could track down a time that he did call, to match the phone number with the one that she had. It happened so infrequently, that she was unable to find the last time that he had called. Several weeks later, in a case of desperation, she decided to take a ride to Lexmark to speak with them personally. Reaching the parking lot, she felt a lump in her throat, and a knot in her stomach, when she pulled in, and her 2012 black Elantra was the only car in the lot. She parked right up front, got out of the car, and walked to the main entrance. She pulled the door to open it. It was locked. What started as confusion, now grew into concern. It was a Wednesday, the middle of the work week at 3pm. Why would they be closed? She placed her left and right hands on each side of her face to block the sun, and pressed her face into the clear glass to take a look. Everything looked normal, but no one was in the building, and all of the lights were turned off. She pulled the door in frustration. Still locked.

"Damn it! What the hell is going on?" she asked out loud.

She walked around the side of the building, looking for any sign of life. She caught a quick glimpse of a middle-aged man walking. He turned the corner and disappeared.

"HEY!" she shouted. "I have something to ask you." No answer. She began running in his direction, still yelling. "Excuse me, sir. I have something to ask you." Carol turned the corner, and ran right into him, almost tripping over him. He was sitting on the ground with a cardboard sign that read in big bold letters, Please give me money. I am a veteran, and don't have a place to live.

"Hey lady. Can you spare a dollar? I don't need much."

Carol stood dumbfounded for several seconds, attempting to regain her composure.

"Yeah, sure. Here's a five." as she threw it on the ground in front of the homeless man.

She was actually surprised at this sudden burst of generosity. When Mike was alive, she would admonish him for throwing his money away at something that was obviously a scam. Always the level-headed one, he would say, "A couple of dollars is not going to break me. I hope that if I am ever in this situation, someone will help me. Even if they are lying, I would never envy this lifestyle. Carol could never come up with an argument to combat that. She always thought that Mike would make a great lawyer. The homeless man's voice brought her back to reality.

"Thanks lady. It's greatly appreciated.

"Um, yeah. No problem," she said, obviously distracted. "Hey, I have a question for you. Do you know why there is no one here in the middle of a work day?"

"I don't know, lady. It's been like this for several months. I would say it's been like this since May. There was a time when I would fall asleep under the hot sun, and wake up to $25. No one ever bothered me here. That's why I am still here, hoping they will return soon."

Carol thought back. It was last May when Mike showed up with his new friend 'Robbie'. A sudden chill came over Carol. She visibly shook.

"Hey lady. Are you ok? You don't look so good!"

Carol chuckled at the irony of that statement.

"Yeah, I'm fine," she said, as she dropped another five dollars at the man's feet.

He quickly scooped it up and yelled," Hey, thanks lady. Come back anytime. Bring your friends."

It was too late. Carol was already running back to her car. She desperately wanted answers, but didn't have a clue where to begin.

13

Carol's car turned quickly into her driveway,
startling both Will and Lisa, who were enjoying a
quiet moment on the couch together, snuggling, and
watching an episode of their mutually favorite show,
'Curb Your Enthusiasm'.

"What the hell was that? asked Lisa.

Will jumped off the couch, opened the blinds,
peering out the window.

"It's just my mother."

"Is she alright?" asked Lisa. "She came into the
driveway like a demon from Hell!"

Will opened the front door and yelled,"Hey, mom.
Are you alright?"

It only took a second to realize that everything was
not alright. Carol looked dazed as she stepped out of
the car. A look of care and confusion was not well
hidden on her face.

Will ran to his mother. "Mom. What's wrong?"

Lisa was now outside with Will.

"Hey, Carol. You don't look well. Are you sick?"

Ignoring the questions, Carol blurted out,"Hey, Will.
Do you remember approximately when your father
brought home the 'robot'?

"Um, let me think." He looked up in contemplation.

Lisa broke the silence. "I remember exactly when it
was."

Carol and Will both looked at her incredulously.

"How do you remember that?" asked Will.

"It was the end of May. Your last semester at Fordham had just ended. We were on the phone making plans when your father was unloading the truck."

"Oh, yeah. You're right. Thanks honey."

"What's the big deal about 'Robbie'? Will asked his mother.

Carol went through the entire story of her attempts to call, the empty building, and her encounter with the homeless man.

"Whatever you do, please don't go anywhere near the downstairs office until I get some answers. That goes for the two of you."

"Come on mom........." Will was going to continue until he saw the seriousness on his mother's face. He knew that she had been through alot the last several months, and he had never seen her act so stern in all of his 25 years.

Lisa squeezed Will's shoulder tighter, the sense of fear growing stronger.

"Alright mom. Whatever you say."

I'm serious!"

I know. I haven't even thought about going downstairs since dad's death. It's much too painful."

Carol saw the hurt in her son's face, grabbed him, and hugged him tightly. Lisa joined in.

Will broke the silence with, "Come watch some 'Curb Your Enthusiasm' with us. I'll put on your favorite episode. The Michael J. Fox episode always makes you laugh."

26

That is true," laughed Carol, wiping away a tear.
Maybe some other time. You two kids have a good
time."

"Well, if you change your mind, you know where to
find us," said Lisa.

Carol walked upstairs to her bedroom, as Will hit the
pause button on the DVD player.

Lisa whispered, "I know your mom has been through
hell, but I thought she was finally starting to get
better. What do you think about what she said?"

I'm not sure, but I need to find out. I already lost my
father. I can't lose my mother as well."

Lisa snuggled with him on the couch, as they both
quietly finished another episode of 'Curb'.

14

Later that night, hours after Lisa had gone home, Will began tossing and turning in his bed. The conversation with his mother brought feelings back to the surface that he had safely tucked away after his father's death. Sadness crept back up into his consciousness, as memories of his father kept him awake. Even on a good night he had difficulty sleeping. He began taking the sleeping supplement Melatonin regularly for the last several years. What began as one 3 milligram pill, slowly escalated into three pills of 10 milligrams. Tonight, he was adding a 4th pill. Anxiety would not allow even 40 milligrams of melatonin to do its job of putting him to sleep. Will continued tossing and turning. Normally he felt most comfortable sleeping on his left side. Tonight, the beating of his heart kept him awake. For some odd reason that he couldn't explain, Will felt like his heart was going to come beating right out of his chest. He finally settled with sleeping on his back. That made it even worse. He just stared at the ceiling. He felt compelled to go downstairs to check on 'Robbie'. He couldn't explain this sudden compulsion. Not once since his father's death was that even a thought, but something his mother said earlier that day triggered his compulsion. He felt bad, even guilty, due to the fact that he specifically told his mother that he would never go downstairs. At the time, he meant every word. Will looked at the digital clock on his nightstand. It read 1:15AM. He sighed, and closed his eyes. He turned to his right side. The need to go downstairs grew stronger. Finally, he jumped out of bed, as if in a trance, and began as quietly as he could to the cellar door that led to the stairway.

"Sorry, mom," said Will, as if she could hear him.

15

Will knew that he needed to be extra careful. Everything that his mother had been through, the worst thing that he could do is add more unneeded stress. Her room was directly across from the cellar door, and she was notorious for being an extremely light sleeper.

Will grabbed his phone. The flashlight app was much better than flicking the light switch. Slowly, he opened the cellar door. Moving very slowly, and gingerly, he placed one foot at a time on each step. Every step made a loud creaking noise. He would stop, cringe at the sound, and look around to ensure that his mother was not awakened. He had made it to the 2nd to the last step. Being so close to the end made him much more comfortable, and confident. He turned off the flashlight app, and placed the phone in his back pocket. As he reached the last step, his phone began to ring from his back pocket. The ring startled him so much that he missed the step, falling on the floor in the process.

"Shit!" he whispered in pain.

Will could now hear rustling from upstairs. His mother's bedroom door opened, and as he lies at the bottom of the stairs, he could now see that the hall light was turned on. .

"Hello, Will. Is that you? asked a concerned Carol from upstairs.

Will regained his senses, jumped up, and hid in a corner.

"Will, honey. Are you alright?"

He wisely didn't answer. Instead he continued hiding in the corner as Carol opened the cellar door, turned on the light, and once again called Will's name. She stopped at the third step, and said,"Will. Are you down there?"

She waited several seconds for an answer, which seemed like an eternity to Will. Satisfied that no one was downstairs, she turned off the light, and closed the door. Feeling somewhat relieved, he sat at the bottom of the stairs, catching his breath, and waiting for his mother to go to bed. In the meantime, he took out his phone to see who his late-night caller was. His phone read: MISSED CALL FROM LISA. He texted back: Sorry. Can't talk right now. I'll explain tomorrow. I Love You. A text immediately came back: I Love you, too. Goodnight. She added a red emoji heart with the text.

16

The light in the hallway was turned off. He waited until he heard his mother shut her bedroom door. Once that happened, he waited an extra minute to ensure that she would be staying there for the remainder of the night.

"I guess this will have to wait until another time," Will said to himself.

The next morning Will woke up feeling groggy. He looked at his clock through bleary eyes. 9:15am.

"DAMN! This is going to be one long-assed day!"

Will dragged himself out of bed to the kitchen. There, Carol sat at the table in her lavender robe, with both hands firmly wrapped around a hot mug of java. She looked even worse than he felt.

"Good Morning, son. I hope you were able to get some sleep."

"Yeah, I'm fine. I should be asking you the same thing."

It was a rough night," Carol answered back. "With everything that happened yesterday, I could barely sleep. I also heard noises late at night. Did you hear anything?"

Will shook his head silently, trying his best not to look guilty.

"I guess it's my overactive imagination. I've been so stressed lately."

Carol continued talking. "I just found out that your

father's life insurance policy is considered null and void."

"Why?" asked Will. How could that happen?"

I guess there is a clause that states that if you commit suicide within 2 years of purchasing the policy, they cancel it. Believe it or not, there are some people that become so desperate, that they purchase life insurance for the sole purpose of offing themselves, and leaving the money to their family."

Carol's eyes began to water. "Your father would NEVER do that! For one thing, we were living very comfortably, and secondly, I will never accept the fact that he was so depressed to contemplate suicide."

At that, she finally broke down. "Oh God. What are we going to do?"

She placed her arms on the kitchen table, and rested her head in them. She began sobbing. Will bent down to hug her.

"It's been rough for all of us. I'll do whatever I can to help."

Carol stopped sobbing, lifting her head up, wiping her nose and eyes on her bathrobe sleeve.

"I was offered a job," she said between sniffles. "It's only 3 days a week, but the extra money will help. Unfortunately, it's from 11pm-7am"

Will sat in stunned silence for a moment. "When did all of this happen?" he asked.

"Bob, our next-door neighbor, works at a factory. He mentioned to me that there was an immediate opening on second shift. He said that I could begin working on Monday."

Today's Saturday. That was quick," said Will.

"I know. I know, but what else can do?"

Will comforted his mother once again, and said, "I could take a semester or two off from Fordham, and find a job to help as well."

Even as the words were coming out of his mouth, Will couldn't understand why, but when all he should be thinking about is helping his mother, and how his father's death has affected everyone, the one thought that was on his mind was, 'Now I will have more time to spend downstairs with 'Robbie'.

"You're the best. Thank you, son. I don't think that will be necessary, but the offer means the world to me," said Carol.

A large, almost sinister, grin appeared on Will's face as he held his mother to his chest.

17

The weekend couldn't end fast enough for Will. He kept busy, and acted like nothing was wrong, but all of Friday night through Sunday, his only thought was 'Once mom goes to work, I can go downstairs'.

He continued reasoning with himself why he suddenly had this irresistible urge to be downstairs, but nothing made seemed to make sense. He was just beginning the healing process over his father's death. Why would he want to open old wounds?

Finally, Monday afternoon arrived. He was in his room watching Netflix on his computer. The latest season of 'House of Cards' had just started, and he couldn't wait to savor all 13 episodes. Frank Underwood, played superbly by Kevin Spacey, had just attempted to kill a member of his Administration, when he heard a soft knock at his bedroom door. He turned around in his swivel chair to see his mother standing in the doorway, looking tired, sad, and excited, all at once.

"On your way to your first day of work?" asked a somewhat anxious Will.

"Yes. I'm a little nervous, only because it's been years since I had a job, but I am also excited to get out of the house for once."

In a mocking tone, Will waved his hand, and said in his most sarcastic tone, " Go on and have some fun, you crazy kid."

That made Carol laugh. "Alright. I'll see you once the shift is done. I will see you in the morning."

Will heard the downstairs door open and close. He went to his window to see his mother driving out of the driveway, and down the street. He went back to watching 'House of Cards'. The show was better than ever, but he couldn't concentrate. All he could think about was 'Robbie the Robot', as if it was taunting him. He noticed that he still had 35 minutes left on the most recent episode. Sighing, he exited out of Netflix, stood up from his chair, and made his way to the downstairs office. He realized that he was silently creeping towards the door. That brought about a laugh.

"Why the hell am I sneaking around? I'm the only one here!"

Will ran down the stairwell, taking 2 steps at a time. "No tripping this time!"

He turned the doorknob to the office. It was locked. "'Damn it!"

Will then remembered that his mother had taken the key, and kept it in her bedroom, after finding his father slumped over with a mysterious hole in his temple.

"Please still be there!" Will said to himself, as he ran up the stairs to his mother's room. He opened several drawers of her dresser. NOTHING! He moved some clothes around, hoping that it would be hidden underneath. NOTHING! He did the same thing with the remaining drawers. His anxiety level skyrocketed as he searched for the key.

He began to worry that she had taken the key with her. He was about to give up, and began walking out the door, when he realized that he never checked the nightstand. Now excited again, he ripped open the nightstand door. It was filled with old receipts, jewelry, and miscellaneous junk. Pushing the receipts and jewelry to the side, Will came across a small envelope. He picked it up, and began feeling the contents. It felt like a key. Excitedly, he ripped the envelope in half. A small key dropped to the floor. He picked it up, running downstairs, hoping, no, praying, that it was the correct key. He inserted the key, turned the knob. It opened!

18

Inside the office, the room was pitch black. He began feeling around for the light switch. He found it, and flicked the switch. The room had not been touched since his father was taken out on a stretcher.

'Robbie' was covered with a blue tarp. Will attempted to pull it off. It was stuck on something. He began pulling harder. Afraid that he was going to break something, he walked over to the other side, lifted the tarp, and threw it in the corner on the floor.

"No wonder dad was obsessed with this 'robot'. This thing is awesome!"

Will caught himself with that last statement. He knew that his parents were the grammar police, and they would be horrified to hear a Fordham student using the word awesome. He began walking around the 'robot', caressing it, almost mesmerized. He stopped, and just stared at it, still not knowing why 'Robbie' was having this kind of effect on him. He looked down, and saw an unplugged cord.

"Ureka!"

Will picked up the cord, and plugged it in. At first nothing happened. He began playing with the cord, pushing it in, ensuring that there was a connection. Suddenly, he heard a humming noise emanating from 'Robbie'. Will stood silently in anticipation. It continued humming, along with a loud clanking noise. One of the four arms that held the needle needed to draw the portraits, swung wildly to the left. The second arm swung clumsily to the right, nearly hitting each other. The 3rd and 4th arms swung as well. After 15 seconds of watching 'Robbie' swing its arms like an octopus with a severe case of Parkinson's, they instantly moved into the straight-ahead position, and stopped. Will didn't move; still stunned, and in awe. He noticed a stack of papers on his father's desk. Excitedly, he grabbed it, and placed it under the only arm that didn't have paper under it. The arm came down quickly, hitting the paper with force. Will wisely moved out of the way. The arm bounced up to the starting position, and stopped. The machine began humming again. The arm came down again, this time much slower. To Will's astonishment, it began drawing a portrait. Will stood transfixed at what was happening. First it drew an outline in black ink. The arm came up again, and the cartridge with blue ink replaced the black. The blue ink was used to color the eyes. Once that was done, the ink cartridge was changed to skin tone, coloring in the face. It took several seconds after the skin was penciled in that Will realized the portrait was of himself. The likeness was unbelievable. He was even more impressed with the facial expression that it gave him. It was an excited look, with his mouth open wide. It reminded him of every picture that he had taken on a rollercoaster. 'Robbie' finished the final touches, the arm came up, and the machine stopped. A sudden burst of energy, and extreme happiness coarsed through Will's body. He suddenly felt extremely happy and alive.

'Where did this sudden burst of energy come from'? Will thought to himself.

He suddenly felt the need to do something. He was much too hyper to stay home and finish 'House of Cards'. He needed to do SOMETHING! He took out his phone to text Lisa. He noticed that it was 1:30am in the morning.

"Damn! I didn't realize that I have been down here that long. I'm sure she is dead to the world."

Will went back to his computer, and began watching 'House of Cards' once again. He was too antsy to enjoy it.

"I need to get out of here NOW!" he exclaimed.

The one problem that Will never encountered was boredom. No matter the time, no matter the day, Will always found something to do. One of his biggest pet peeves was listening to people whine how there was nothing to do. He was never afraid to venture off on his own. Sometimes, he preferred it. Tonight, would prove not to be an exception. With the time now reading 1:37am; a sudden burst of energy, and extreme happiness, Will grabbed his I-POD, downloaded 3 of his favorite podcasts, Gilbert Gottfried's Amazing Colossal Podcast being one of them, got in his car, drove to the nearest 24-hour Dunkin Donuts, grabbed a large, all black coffee, and began driving aimlessly. He didn't have a set destination, but with a large coffee in his hand, and a hilarious interview with Tony Orlando playing on his

I-POD, he didn't care. There was no way he could sit at home with all of his restless energy. He made it to the highway, and began his adventure to NO WHERE! He didn't understand why, but he couldn't remember ever feeling this alive. He thought about what could be causing this major shift with his emotions, but, as if possessed, he decided he could care less. Will felt the phone buzzing from his back pocket. Holding the coffee with his right hand, and steering the car with his left knee, he reached into his back pocket with his left hand to grab the phone. He saw the 8 red and purple hearts, combined with 5 yellow emoji's blowing kisses. It was a text from Lisa. "It's 2:15 in the morning. Why is she still up?" Will asked out loud.

Without hesitation, he put his phone on blue tooth, and dialed her cell. Lisa answered on the 2nd ring.

"Lisa Lisa and the Cult Jam," screamed Will.

"WOW! Why are you so excited, and where the hell are you?"

"I can't explain it. The Godfather of Soul put it best when he coined the phrase, "I FEEL GOOD!"

"Who is this impostor, and what have you done with Will?" Lisa shot back, only half-joking. "I've never heard you this happy, especially recently."

Will was silent for several seconds. Lisa, realizing that maybe she shouldn't have brought up the most recent events, attempted to apologize.

"I'm so sorry, babe," she said. "I didn't mean to bring up such a sore subject. It's just so great to hear you sound so ALIVE!!"

"Not a problem at all!   Wanna go for a ride?"

Now? You're nuts! It's going on 3am."

"Yeah, I know. I'm just too hyper to stay home."

As much as I love you, I think I'll pass. Unlike some people, I need to get up for work tomorrow."

"Alright. Your loss. What time do you leave work?"

"4pm," said Lisa.

"Great! I'll pick you up at 4:10. Goodnight."

Before Lisa could respond, Will had disconnected the call.

"Now, back to the podcast."

As Lisa went back to sleep, Will drove around for another hour and a half. His phone read 3:45am as he pulled into the driveway. He still couldn't understand why he still felt so happy and excited. The rest of the night was spent staring at the ceiling.

19

He jumped out of bed when he heard his mother's keys in the door. Running to the door, he opened it before his mother could get it open with the key.

"Hey, how was your first day? Did you like it? I'm sure you were the best employee.

"Whoa, whoa, whoa," said Carol. What's gotten into you?"

"Nothing. I'm just so happy to see the World's Greatest Mom!"

"Alright. Now I know something is seriously wrong," Carol said sarcastically. "How many cups, or should I say gallons of coffee did you drink?"

"None. This is just my natural, warm, bubbly personality."

Carol mockingly checked her wrist for a pulse.

"I must have died and gone to heaven to receive such a warm welcome."

"No, you are stuck here in Hell with me," joked Will. Let's get some breakfast. I'm cooking."

"If Allen Funt was still alive, I would swear this was 'Candid Camera'."

"No, mom. You have not been 'PUNKED'!"

Will prepared breakfast, while Carol went upstairs to take a shower. She came downstairs 20 minutes later to the fine country smell of eggs, bacon, a slice of sausage, and 2 pieces of Italian toast.

"Sit right here, my Queen," said Will as he pulled out a kitchen chair for his mother.

"I don't know which pod person you are, but I could get used to this very quickly."

"I can't explain it, but late last night........."

Will stopped, realizing that he almost inadvertently admitted to going downstairs, after he promised that he wouldn't. He quickly regained his composure.

"I just decided that it's time to stop feeling sorry for myself, and instead of mourning the people in my life that are gone, I should begin enjoying my life with the people that are still with me."

Carol's eyes began to water. She pushed her chair out, stood up, grabbed Will, and gave him a huge hug.

"I love you so much, my son. I know how tough it's been on all of us, but you are exactly right. I need to start living again, myself. I'll always miss your father, and a day will never go by when I won't stop thinking of him, but I need to follow your example."

She hugged him even tighter. Will broke the silence.

"Let's not turn this into a 'Terms of Endearment' remake. I'm picking up Lisa at 4. Let's do something."

"Sorry, son. I wish I had just an ounce of your energy. You two have a great time. I'm going to get some much-needed sleep."

Carol went upstairs to bed. Within 30 seconds of her head hitting the pillow, she was out like a light. Even though Will didn't sleep a wink, he was still full of energy. The compulsion hit him once again, this time even harder than last night.

"Time to go downstairs to play with my good friend 'Robbie the Robot'" He called upstairs. "Goodnight mom."

20

Knowing that his mom is a light sleeper, Will quietly
crept downstairs. He was happy that he forgot to
lock the door. He opened the door, and the humming
sound signaling 'Robbie' coming to life, instantly
began. He looked at the cord plugged neatly into the
socket.

"That's funny. I'm could have sworn that I unplugged
it before I went upstairs."

The arm on the first machine came down hard,
hitting the stack of paper that Will had left on the
machine. It began drawing a portrait of Will once
again smiling, looking energetic and happy. The
second arm hit the paper. It began drawing a portrait
of Will as well. This portrait had Will looking much
more somber. Without warning, his emotions
instantly changed. He no longer felt extremely
happy. His energy had completely dissipated as well.
He wasn't depressed, but a slight feeling of
melancholy replaced his happy demeanor. It
happened so fast that Will had to sit back in the
office chair. The sudden change in emotions left him
feeling weak, and dizzy. The third and fourth arms of
his good friend 'Robbie' began drawing portraits. The
third showed a curling of his lip, creating a sneer. A
feeling of anxiousness was now added to the
equation. The fourth arm had just finished. Will went
over to pick up the portrait. It was him alright, but
the slight sneer had now turned into a picture of
disgust. His eyebrows were narrow, and his lips were

curled. He immediately felt angry, irate, annoyed, cross, indignant, and irked. Without reason, he suddenly wanted to lash out at anyone or anything. He grabbed the remaining three portraits from the machine, and began tearing them up. It didn't make him feel any better. He actually felt angrier. He swung around one of the arms. It did a complete 360 and hit Will in the head.

"You stupid motherfucker!" he yelled as he kicked 'Robbie'. The machine let out a loud whining noise. "FUCK YOU!!!"

Will kicked it again. This time the machine went silent. He now heard the shuffling of feet upstairs.

"Oh, great. Now mom's up!"

21

Less than 30 minutes ago, Will would do whatever it took to conceal his whereabouts. His intense anger, mixed with extreme hatred, and apathy, left him uncaring. For a reason, he couldn't even begin to explain, this anger was now aimed at his mother. Carol opened the door and yelled," Will, honey. Are you downstairs?"

"Yeah. What are you going to do, ground me?" Will muttered under his breath.

Carol asked again, "Will, sweetheart. Is that you?" She was now walking downstairs. Will walked out of the office, and slammed the door shut.

"Yeah, I'm down here. What's it to you?"

Carol was shocked. Will NEVER disrespected her like that. She always bragged to her friends, and anyone that was willing to listen, that she was the luckiest mom in the world, because she had the best son. He never went through that weird phase that most teenagers experience when they don't want anything to do with their parents. He never had that 'too cool for mom and dad' phase.

She stood in the middle of the stairwell dumbfounded. Will shot back from the bottom of the staircase, "Are you just going to stand there all day, or are you going to fucking move so I could go to my room?"

That snapped her out of it.

"Will, why are you so angry? What caused this sudden mood swing? Just 2 hours ago, you were the happiest person alive."

With total disdain, Will walked up the stairs, pushing his mother to the side. "Can't a guy have a bad day?" Carol grabbed the railing to catch her balance. As she turned around to address him, he slammed the upstairs door. Carol ran after Will. He was running upstairs to his room, two steps at a time. She was behind him yelling, "I know you have been through alot, but that does not give you the right to disrespect me!"

He responded by slamming his bedroom door shut. From the other side of the door Will said, "I thought you were tired. Get some sleep."

Carol began sobbing heavily. "I went through this with your father, towards the end. I will not go through this again, with my one and only son."

Will turned on his stereo. Carol's words were drowned out by Pat Benatar's classic, 'Hit Me With Your Best Shot'. She began pounding on the door, her shock and sadness now replaced with anger. "Will. You open the door this very minute!"

The music became louder. Pat Benatar's booming voice was all she heard. It was if she was being taunted by her lyrics. 'Hit me with your best shot. FIRE AWAY'!!!!!!!

49

Realizing that any attempt to reason with her son at this point was futile, she did what she always does when depressed: go downstairs to watch 'reality' tv. Will threw the CD cover at the door. Normally, he would be able to reason with himself, coming to the conclusion that life wasn't so bad after all, lifting him out of his bad mood. Today was different; MUCH DIFFERENT. He couldn't remember ever feeling such intense anger, and hatred. He stayed in his room all day, only leaving twice to use the bathroom down the hall. Both times he heard his mother yelling up to him from the downstairs couch, "Will, come down here. I need to speak with you."

Both times he purposely slammed the bathroom and bedroom door shut, making it clear that he had no interest in speaking with her. Hours later, he heard a knock at his bedroom door.

"Will. You obviously have zero interest in speaking with me, but Lisa is here. She said you were supposed to pick her up after work. That was an hour and a half ago."

"Shit!" he muttered to himself, as he checked the time on his phone. "Tell her I'm not here," he said barely audible over the music.

"What was that?" asked Carol.

Will turned down the music, and yelled, "I said, tell her I'm not here!"

"Will. It's me, Lisa. I know you are here. Why did you blow me off?"

"Go away. I'm not in the mood for company right now."

Lisa's usually small, indecisive voice suddenly became louder, bellowing confidence. "I don't know what your problem is, and frankly, at this point I could care less. You will not talk to me, your mother, or anyone else like that. I refuse to leave until you open this door, and explain yourself."

"Good luck honey," said Carol. She gave Lisa a hug, and walked back downstairs. Lisa became more defiant. She began pounding her fists on the door. "We can do this all day and night. I am NOT going anywhere!"

No response from Will. She kicked and pounded the door. Lisa's anger was mixed with empathy.

"I know what your father's death has crippled you emotionally, but I can't understand how you can go from one extreme to the next in a matter of a few hours. Secondly, we had a deal that we would always be there for each other. Do you think that you are the only one that is hurting? Don't shut me out."

She heard some rustling of feet on the other side of the door. The music was turned down even lower, and she saw the doorknob begin to turn. Will opened the door, flinging it open with full-force. The doorknob slammed into Lisa's right shoulder. She began massaging her right shoulder with her left hand, as she watched Will walk back into his room, sitting on his bed, without a care for what he did.

51

The anger now overshadowed any empathy she previously had for Will.

"How can anyone that is always so loving, turn into a belligerent asshole so quickly?" she asked incredulously.

This took Will by surprise. In all of the years that they were together, she never swore at him, let alone raise her voice.

"I'm the asshole? I'm the fucking asshole? Will repeated a second time.

Lisa felt an overwhelming sensation of fear, anxiety, and anger. She felt like she was provoking a wild bear in the woods. She never saw this dark side, and wasn't quite sure how to handle it. Instead of engaging in a war of words, she decided that diplomacy was her best source of action. She walked over to the bed, sat next to him; putting her arm around him.

"Will, I'm not sure what is causing this Dr. Jeckyl/Mr. Hyde moment, but I know this is not who you are. You are a sweet, loving, and kind person who would never hurt a fly."

Her calming voice seemed to make Will even angrier. He grabbed her arm, ripping it off his shoulder.

"What the fuck do you know about me, you clueless bitch?"

Lisa's back and forth patience and understanding completely slipped away. She responded, "Well, I do know that I refuse to be with someone that treats me with a total lack of respect. Your Linda Blair head-spinning, pea soup spitting moment is not only hurtful, but tiring. If you want to stay an asshole, then the only girlfriend you will have is your left hand. Have fun pounding your potato!"

Lisa stood up, and began walking towards the door. Will stood up, opened the door, and pushed her out into the hallway, once again hitting her bruised right shoulder. Lisa looked at her shoulder, then looked up at him. This had finally put her over the edge.

"That's it, you low-life piece of shit! You will NEVER lay your hands on me again, because you will NEVER see me again! Have fun sitting in your dark room, isolating yourself from everyone that ever cared about you."

Will slammed the door shut in disgust, without saying a word. Lisa began sobbing loudly. She ran down the stairs to the front door. Carol grabbed her, wrapped her arms around her, attempting to calm her down. Lisa tried to break away. Carol held on to her tighter.

"It's alright, sweetheart. Calm down."

They were both crying now.

Lisa stopped fighting to break away. She was still sobbing heavily, and began convulsing, as she spoke incoherently about Will.

"Lisa. Lisa. Calm down. I can't understand a word you are saying. You're safe now. No one is going to hurt you. I promise."

Carol walked Lisa to the couch. It took several minutes, but she was finally able to calm Lisa down enough to where she could explain what happened upstairs.

"What's wrong with him? I have never seen that side of him."

Carol wiped some tears from her left cheek. "I know. I don't know what's happening. His father had the same severe mood swings towards the end of his life. I have never seen such swift changed in moods. I feel so helpless."

Carol and Lisa sat on the couch, talking, and weeping for the next 20 minutes. Lisa stood up, and told Carol that she had to go.

"I hope you two can work it out," said Carol.

"Unless he gives me a sincere apology, I'm afraid that it will never be the same," responded Lisa.

Carol understood, and realized that the best response to that was no response. She let Lisa out, and closed the door. She looked up to the top of the stairs where Will was holing himself up in his room, and sighed. She walked up the stairs to his room, and knocked on the door. As she expected, there was no response.

"I hope you know that you are pushing away everyone that cares about you. If you don't apologize to Lisa, you are going to lose her forever. I hope you come to your senses before it's too late."

Not expecting any response, she added, "I need to get some things done before work. I hope that when

I come back in the morning, I find the sweet, loving son that I have known for a quarter of a century." With that, Carol walked away, changed into her work clothes, grabbed her purse, and walked out the door. Still seething, he waited until his mother had pulled out of the driveway, and walked downstairs to the office.

22

As if on cue, he opened the door, and the machine began humming. One of the arms started moving, then the second, third, and finally the last.

"Fuck You!" he said to 'Robbie' as he smacked one of the arms with the palm of his right hand. He realized that he had loosened it. He hit it again, this time harder. It became even more loose, and began to wobble. One more hit with his palm, and the arm fell to the floor.

"3 more to go!"

He did the same to the second arm. As Will was preparing to break off the third arm, it suddenly jerked violently, hitting the pile of blank paper underneath it. Will felt a sharp pain in his forehead. The arm jolted back up, and came down full-force, hitting the paper. He felt another sharp pain on his left cheek.

"What the hell?" Will asked himself, placing his left hand where he felt the pain on his left cheek.

The arm jolted up and down once again. This time the pain emanated from his right cheek.

"Motherfucker!"

Will placed his hand on his right cheek. He felt something warm. He opened his hand to look. A small drop of blood was in the palm of his hand. The arm dropped again. This time he felt a sharp pain on his chin. He touched his chin, once again finding blood. Will felt a sudden rush of dizziness come over him. He sat down in the chair to catch himself from passing out.

The arm came up and down, hitting the paper harder each time. Blood began dripping from his left temple. The arm was now moving at an incredible speed, up and down, up and down. The pain seemed to be concentrating on only one spot: his left temple. To Will, it felt like a drill was penetrating his skull. Blood was now pouring from his temple like a faucet, as 'Robbie's' arm moved up and down at speeds that Will had never seen before. He lifted his shirt up to his temple. The bottom of the shirt became instantly soaked in blood. Will was beginning to lose consciousness. Four more motions of the arm going up and down caused Will to slump over; his head hitting the desk.

The arm stopped moving, going back to its neutral position. The machine turned off. Will's head lay flat on its right side, with blood still flowing from the left temple. Saliva was now forming at the corner of his mouth, while his pants were now stained with piss and shit. Will stayed that way until his mother came home from work early in the A.M.

23

The clock read 6:56AM at the factory. Carol was anxious to leave work. She had slipped back into the depression that she was slowly creeping out of. Will's sudden and extreme change in personality was too much for her to handle. She couldn't understand what was happening. Several months ago, she had the perfect family. A great husband and father that actually loved spending time with his family. She knew that many of her friends envied her. A majority of her friend's husbands only spoke when they asked if dinner was ready, and instead of eating with the family, plopped themselves in front of the television set to watch mindless shows.

Just several months ago, she had the perfect son: smart, good-looking, funny, and just like his father, never a sign of a temper or depression. Now, she had lost her husband to severe mood swings, and Will was now on the fast track to meeting his father. Carol was determined NOT to let that happen again. She may have lost a husband, but she would be damned to let Will spiral downward the same way. The clock now read 7:00am. She punched out, and walked rapidly to her car. She wanted to get home quickly, and shake some sense into Will, letting him know how much he is loved. She started the car, put it into reverse, pulled out of the parking lot, and began the 20-minute ride home. She turned on the radio, hoping it would help drown out her thoughts, and calm her down. As if mocking her, Pat Benatar began belting out the chorus of 'Hit Me With Your Best Shot'. As Benatar once again instructed Carol to 'FIRE AWAY', she hit the knob on her steering wheel that changed the station, and yelled, "Fire Away At This BITCH!!!" With that she turned the station to the mellower, but still great, 'Love Me Tender', as sung by The King, Elvis Presley. This made her sad, as she let the lyrics soak in. She turned the station again. George Michael began to tell her that she needed to have 'Faith'.

"What the hell? Is the radio now personally speaking to me?" mused Carol.

She turned the radio off, deciding that Silence would be Golden for the remainder of the ride home.

17 minutes later, she parked her car in the driveway. She was surprised, and somewhat startled, that all of the lights were off, including the porch light. Even though it was morning, Will always left the light on for her. He would usually make a Motel 6 reference, and they would both laugh.

Carol jumped out of the car, not even bothering to close the door. She opened the screen door, and began furiously searching for the house key.

Nervously, she fumbled them several times, before she stopped herself, took a deep breath, gained her composure, and said to herself, "Time to calm down. He's probably fast asleep."

She found the correct key, opened the door; looking around the house as she entered. It was eerily quiet.

59

It was still early, but Will was always an early riser, even if he had a late night. He often bragged that he was able to accomplish so much during the day because he   only needed 4-5 hours of sleep. After yesterday's debacle, she needed to resolve the matter immediately.

"Will. Will, honey. Where are you? Sorry to wake you, but we need to talk. It's killing me how we left things."

She walked upstairs to his bedroom. The door was closed. She quietly opened it, whispering, "Will. Sorry to wake you, but....."

Carol stopped dead in her tracks. The bed was empty. The fear and anxiety went into overdrive. She began walking down the hall, checking the bathroom, and the other bedroom. She was now screaming, "Will. Where are you? It's not funny. Tell me where you are."

She walked back downstairs, checking the kitchen, and living room. NOTHING. She was in full panic mode when she noticed that the door leading downstairs to the office was slightly ajar. She noticed that the light from the office was turned on. Carol flung the door open, nearly ripping it off its hinges, as she ran downstairs. Anger was now mixed in with fear.

"Will! I told you NEVER to go anywhere near this office. I thought you were too old to be grounded, but I guess I was wrong. I will not stand for the complete disrespect you are showing me."

She meant what she was saying, but it was mostly fueled by fear. She saw that the office door was open, with the light on, but was also terrified of what she would find. Carol jumped the final step, turned the corner, grabbed the door handle, swinging herself into the office.

"Will Robertson, answer me for Christ's sake!"

With that last statement, she saw what she dreaded most. It was Will, slumped over in the office chair, his head resting on the desk. His jaw was open, blood spilling out from the right corner of his mouth, onto the desk. Without thinking, Carol ran over to her son, and picked up his head. Blood, mixed with fragments of bones and brain, were seeping out of his left temple.

"NOOOOOOOOOO!" Carol screamed. "This can't be happening again!"

She began screaming, and crying hysterically, cradling her dead son in her arms, as blood and small fragments of brain seeped through her shirt. This went on for what seemed like an eternity to Carol, but in reality, was only 10 minutes.

With her voice hoarse, and her tear ducts dried up, a sudden clarity struck her.

"I need to call the police and the paramedics."

With an eerie calmness, Carol gently placed Will's head back on the office desk, took the phone from her back pocket, and began dialing 9-1-1. She dialed 9. The machine began to hum. She stopped dialing, and began staring at the machine known to her husband and son as 'Robbie', as if in shock. The machine became quiet again. She snapped back to reality, and dialed 1. 'Robbie' came back to life. The arm jerked up and down. The phone at her side, she watched as 'Robbie' began drawing a portrait. The common-sense side of her brain told her to dial the last 1, and get the police and paramedics here immediately. Carol wasn't sure what was happening to her, but she felt paralyzed as it continued to draw. She also felt as if all emotions were being drained from her body. She stood there transfixed, as the machine began adding more details. It became clear that the portrait was of her. She continued to feel numb; no sadness, anger, or happiness. Apathy wasn't even a strong enough word to describe what she felt.

Suddenly, the arm swung down again, filling in the details of her mouth. The portrait now featured Carol grinning from ear to ear. That very instant, she felt a sense of extreme happiness. Not even the sight of Will's lifeless body could wipe the smile off of her face. The arm jerked upward back into the neutral mode. The machine stopped humming, and was now off.

24

Carol began staring at the portrait of herself. The feeling of ecstasy became stronger, as the smile on her face increased. She scanned the office, seeing all of the blood, carnage, and pieces of brain strewn about the room. She grabbed the portrait from the machine, and began staring at it adoringly. She hit the red button on her cell, ending the call she started, and put the phone back in her pocket. "Time to hang this masterpiece in the living room," Carol said to herself, laughing, as she walked up the stairs, and closed the door. She couldn't explain why, but she knew that now EVERYTHING WAS GOING TO BE ALRIGHT!!!!!

THE END

CAN'T CATCH A *BRAKE*

It was a beautiful spring day in the middle of April. Not a cloud in the sky. It was the first time the thermometer read 70 degrees since last September. Twenty-four-year-old Alex Larson was awakened by the birds chirping outside his open window. He knew instantly that it was going to be a great day. And why not? He was young, good looking, cocky, arrogant, and best of all, his parents were rich. They were either incredibly smart, or just plain lucky, playing the stock market back in the 80's. He wasn't sure which one it was. He didn't care, because he was now reaping the benefits. Anyone looking outside at his high school graduation present would agree. Outside in the driveway was a 2008 Red Corvette. Sure, it was a 2008 hand-me-down from his father. His dad ensured that he always had the nicest, best, and most importantly, newest 'toys'. He bought the latest model, leaving his only child his used 2008 car. Used was tough to describe the car. It may have been several years old, but his father only racked up 8,000 miles. He always had a reason for not driving it: It was too cold. It was too hot. It was too windy. There was too much traffic. The list went on and on. Alex would definitely not have that problem. He was always looking for a reason to take the car out for a spin. No matter where he was headed, he always made sure to drive by the hottest girl in townhouse, Sally Cuccaro. He lived in the small Connecticut town of Wolcott. With a population of 16,000 mostly older folks, it was easy for her to stand out from the rest. Twenty-two years old, long, wavy blond hair, and even longer legs, she looked great in a two-piece bikini. Hell, she would look great wearing a paper bag! Alex had a crush on her ever since the 7th grade. She loved flirting, but always turned away his advances. It wasn't until he received his graduation present that she decided to go on a date with him. A part of Alex knew that the car was the only reason she decided to say yes, but his arrogance wouldn't allow him to believe it. He figured once she got to know him, she would become putty in his hands.

2

Alex jumped out of bed, feeling refreshed. He
normally had a tough time getting up in the morning,
hitting the snooze button 3 or 4 times before
actually dragging himself out of bed. For some
reason, today was different. Leaving the window and
shade open, allowing the sunlight, along with the
warm breeze most likely played a huge factor. He sat
up in bed, matting down his short, somewhat curly
black hair. He could never understand how people
took showers at night. Besides the fact that it helped
wake him up, that was the ONLY way to get rid of
the dreaded 'bed-head' that he encountered every
morning. He jumped out of bed to make his way to
the bathroom, when a glare from his bedroom
window stopped him in his tracks. There it was in all
its glory: his freshly washed and waxed 2008 Red
Corvette. He held up his left hand to shield his eyes.
No matter how long he had it, he was always
transfixed by its beauty. It was Sleek, Fast, and
Formidable. The digital clock that he had on his
dresser snapped him back to reality.
"Shit! I have to work today, "he said.
Alex felt that going to college was a stupid idea. Why
should he, or his parents, waste their money on four
years of college, when he knew he was set for life. He

already had a Trust Fund set up, and money would never be an issue. His parents had a different definition of the word responsible. They told him that it was fine if he didn't want to go to college, but he wasn't going to sit home gathering dust, and watching reruns of 'The Jerry Springer Show' all day. He would have to get a full-time job. Alex was never concerned about a career, because he knew it wasn't necessary, so when it came to finding a job, he never gave it much thought. A family friend was a District Manager of Rite-Aid, and he was hired as a cashier on the spot.

3

The clock read 8:30am. He was scheduled
for 10am. He walked out the bedroom, down the
hallway, through the kitchen, and into the bathroom
to get ready. Turning on the shower, he opened up
the bathroom window to let some air in. A warm
breeze from outside flushed over him. That was the
precise moment that Alex made up his mind.
"I'm calling in sick," he said confidently to himself.
He practiced his mock cough several times before
calling. Alex knew it didn't sound believable, but he
didn't care. It was too nice to be stuck at work all
day.
"Today I'm taking 'Spanky' for a ride!"
Spanky was the nickname that he gave his car. It was
a nod to his father's favorite show growing up, which
had become his favorite as well, 'The Little Rascals'.
He made the phone call, doing his best to sound sick.
Alex could sense that they didn't believe him, but he
didn't care. He only had one thing on his mind: take
'Spanky' out on this first nice spring day, of course
driving by Sally's house.
He took his shower, dressed, and was walking out
the door when a cool breeze hit him.
"Maybe it's not as warm as I thought. I better go back
inside to get my spring jacket.
Alex went back inside, grabbed his sweatshirt jacket
from the closet, and headed back to 'Spanky'.

He started the car. It purred like a kitten. He sat there, revving it up, feeling almost orgasmic. He slowly backed out of his parent's driveway, taking a right onto the main road, and began driving. He wasn't sure where his final destination would be, but knew that his first would be driving by Sally's.

"It's too quiet."

Alex turned the radio on. It was already preset to his favorite satellite station, 'The 70's on 7'. He loved everything from the 70's: music, movies, clothing.

"I guess I am an old soul, " said Alex as he began singing along to Foghat's classic, 'Free Ride'.

"Perfect song for today's activities," he added.

4

While driving, Alex heard a clunking sound.

"Fuck that!" he said turning up the volume, and singing even louder.

Thirty seconds later, the clunking became even louder

"What the hell?"

Alex turned off the radio. The clunking noise stopped.

"Great! Maybe I just hit something."

He took a left onto Eden Street, which was Sally's street. He applied the brakes as he made the turn. The clunking returned. He took his foot off the brake. The clunking disappeared. He hit the brake. The clunking reappeared.

"Shit! exclaimed Alex. "Last time this happened I was on my way to Howe Caverns in New York. I ended up ruining the rotors. I can't let 'Spanky' endure the same fate!"

He decided to give it one last test. The clunk reappeared and disappeared once again.

"Off to the mechanic I go," he said in disgust.

The small town of Wolcott only had one mechanic that everyone went to. Come to think of it, this small town only had one of everything: one supermarket, one library, and only one mechanic. His name was Paul. He had his own garage, aptly named Paul's Garage, for as long as Alex could remember. His family had been taking their cars to him for years. He was hoping that a little nepotism might earn him a free check-up.

5

Alex slowed down to a crawl, not wanting to do anymore damage to the brakes. He could see the big blue shop up ahead on his right. He pressed on the gas in anticipation. He looked up to see the traffic light in front of him change from yellow to red.

"Shit!" exclaimed Alex, as he slammed on the brakes. "Shit! Shit! Shit!" he repeated, slamming the steering wheel with his fist, synchronized with the swearing. This time the brakes made a loud popping noise.

"Perfect way to spend my day off!"

The light turned green, and he continued slowly to the parking lot where a big white sign read in bold black letters: PAUL'S GARAGE.   YES, WE'RE OPEN!

"Well, you better damn well be, " Alex muttered.

He pulled the car up to the garage door, parked, got out of the car, and began looking in the garage for Paul. He didn't see anyone.

Alex began to call out, "Paul.   Paul, are you there?" Nothing. A little louder this time. "Paul. I know you, or someone is here. Where the hell are you?"

A door to his left opened up. Paul stepped out. He was in his mid 50's, long black, somewhat grayish hair, tied up in a ponytail, looking like he just fell out of a time machine from 1966. He also had a large beer gut. Looking at all of the empty Budweiser cans lying around, it wasn't too hard to figure out where that came from.

Paul wiped his moist hands on his already greasy shirt and said, "Can't a guy take a shit in peace?"
"Sorry about that, I just....."
Paul interrupted him. "Jesus Christ. Aren't you Tim's boy?"
Alex didn't particularly like being called boy, but for a 'Family Discount', Paul could call him whatever he felt like.
"Yeah. That's me. Tim's boy."
Alex swallowed hard on that last word.
"What seems to be the damage?" asked Paul.
"I'm not sure, but the brakes are making some funky noises. I'm no Five Star Mechanic like yourself, but I'm guessing it's not a good thing."
Paul remained quiet for several seconds, noticing the sarcasm in Alex's voice.
"Bring this car in, and let's see if this Five Star mechanic can get you back on the road."
Alex brought the Corvette in nice and slow, as Paul directed him. He stopped the car, got out, and handed Paul the keys.
Paul jingled the keys in his right hand, as he began looking up and down the fine piece of machinery that stood in front of him.
"Must be nice to be able to afford one of these. I'm lucky if I can make the payments on that load of shit over there, "he said, pointing to his 1995 AMC Concorde. The way business has been lately, I might be living in it, as well as driving it."

Alex sensed that Paul was being condescending. He, just like everyone else in town, knew that his parents had all of the money, not the spoiled little Trust Fund Baby.

Alex shot back with his own brand of sarcasm. "If that's the case, you might want to drive down South. At least it will be warm down there!"

Paul let out a small, humorless chuckle. "At least it will be warm down there, " he repeated. "Yep, that's real funny."

He paused again. Alex was becoming noticeably irritated. A smile appeared on Paul's face. He waited another thirty seconds, knowing that it was bothering Alex. Finally, he said, "Well, let's put this beauty up on the lift, and see what's wrong with it." Alex backed up as Paul started the car.

"Be careful," said Alex.

Paul laughed as he set the car on the lift. He wasn't in the mood to have some snot-nosed rich kid tell him how to run his business. When it was on the lift, Paul used the lug wrench to loosen the bolts, and remove the tires. He went from front to back, left to right, carefully inspecting the brakes before moving to the next tire.

Alex became impatient. "Well, do you see anything?" Paul looked up from his inspection. "Do you want this fixed correctly, or not? Let me do my job. You'll be the first to find out."

Alex held both arms up in surrender. "Alright, alright. I'm going to walk down the street to the diner to get some food."

"That's the best idea I have heard all day. Actually, it's the only idea I heard." He paused, and said, "Well, I guess that still makes it the best!"

Paul laughed a little too hard at his own joke. Alex sighed audibly, and began walking to the small-town diner, the only diner in town, that of course everyone frequented.

6

Alex planned on ordering what he always ordered.
No matter the time of day, his order was always 2
eggs over-easy, 2 sausage patties, home fries, and
Italian toast to round it out. This was washed down
with a large water, and a hot, black coffee.

He wasn't in the socializing mood, so he picked a
booth all the way in the back, knowing the odds were
high that he would run into someone he knew. He
was right. Within 20 minutes he saw his grade school
teacher, his baseball coach, and even the town
mayor made a morning stop. Alex dropped his head,
staring at his meal until they found a seat. 'Just like a
dog', he thought. 'It's smart not to make eye contact.
I'll never get out of here.'

He finished his meal, nursed his coffee, and drank his
water until all that was left was a cup of melting ice.
Looking at the clock on the wall, Alex said,"That's
more than enough time for that mutant from 'The
Hill's Have Eyes' to have my car ready."

He motioned the waitress for the bill, gave her his
credit card, waited for the receipt, and made his way
back to the garage. Walking back, he could now hear
loud music blasting from inside the garage. The
closer he got, he realized it was AC/DC's classic
'Back in Black' blaring from a boom box, situated on a
bench, close to where Paul was working on the car.
"Hey!"

No answer. Alex walked over to the boom box, and turned the volume to zero.

"What the fuck?" asked a confused Paul, as he pulled himself up from underneath the car.

"It was the only way to get your attention. Why the hell are you underneath my car anyway? I thought it was the brakes."

It was the brakes," said Paul, wiping his eternally greasy hands on his severely faded 1980's era AC/DC shirt.

Looking at the shirt, Alex commented, "Hey, man. You have a real hard-on for AC/DC!"

Not batting an eye, Paul shot back, "Best rock band in the world!"

Not exactly impressed with this assessment, Alex said, "Well, let me ask you one more time. If it wasn't the brakes, then what the hell are you doing underneath 'Spanky', I mean my car?"

"Spanky? Aw, now ain't that a cute name for a sports car?"

Paul could sense that Alex was silently seething, so he continued. " Since it's such a nice car, and your father is a great guy, I'm not going to let you leave here without ensuring that this car, oh, I'm sorry, I mean 'Spanky', is in 100% mint driving condition."

Alex detected the sarcasm, and replied in his most condescending tone," Well, thank you, Mr. Mechanic Sir. What would I ever do without you?!"

Paul had visions of punching this spoiled punk in the face, but instead settled for giving him a dirty look. He then walked over to the boom box, turning up the volume full blast, singing along to his favorite song from that disc, 'You Shook Me All Night Long'.

He grabbed the keys off the hook and said, "Alright. That will be $85.00."

Alex's jaw dropped. "What?"

Paul repeated what he said, SLOWER and LOUDER.

"I said, that will be $85.00."

With the boom box blaring, Alex yelled over Brian Johnson's scratchy voice one more time."What?"

Paul turned down the volume himself, and said, "That will be $85.00. I had to replace the back brakes. The front brakes will need to be replaced soon. Will that be cash or credit?"

Alex sighed as he reluctantly took out his credit card, and handed it to Paul. The card was swiped, and the receipt was signed.

"Maybe this $85.00 will pay for a maid to get rid of all your empties."

Paul knew that Alex was attempting to provoke him, but he didn't want to show him that he was getting under his skin. Instead, he smiled and said in a less than sincere tone, "You have a great day. Be careful out there."

'What the hell did he mean by that. Alex kept that thought to himself. He knew that would just begin another boring conversation. He started the car, revved it 2 or three times, and turned up the volume on his radio. As he backed out of the garage, and began driving away, Lynyrd Skynyrd's 'Sweet Home Alabama drowned out whatever Angus Young song Paul was now listening to.

7

"I hope his mechanic skills are much better than his personality. If not, he's fucked!" muttered Alex angrily.

Seeing that it was a weekday afternoon, and most people were either working or in school, Alex had the road to himself. He began to pick up speed. He was up to 45 mph, when he decided to tap the brakes to give them a test. He didn't hear a noise, but they felt weird, almost like it wasn't catching He turned down the radio, sped up, and tapped the brakes again. The clunking noise was still there. He applied the brakes one more time. The Clunking was louder than ever.

"Damn it! I thought Mr. Superstar said he fixed the problem! Well, I'm definitely not taking it back to that incompetent asshole!" Alex continued this conversation with himself. "Since he's such a big fan of my father, I'll have dad get my money back, while I take it to a real mechanic. Until then, I'm going to enjoy my 'sick day.'"

Alex decided he was going to take his car to an old high school friend that was a mechanic in the next town over, but not today. He decided that he would stay close by, instead of wasting several more hours, just to hear that, SURPRISE! SURPRISE!, he needed brakes. While driving and thinking of what to do next, he crossed the town line into the larger, adjoining city of Waterbury. It was much bigger than the small town that he grew up in. Back in its heyday, it was known as The Brass Mill for all of its factory jobs. Now it's sadly known as Sin City. Even though there are still some nice areas, most of it is riddled with low income housing and growing crime rates. The one bright spot was its Barnes and Noble. "If I have to stay close by, I don't mind spending an afternoon reading a good book, while sipping my favorite beverage, The Blueberry Green Tea." Luckily, it was only 2 miles down the road. He turned up the radio to drown out the annoying clunking sound. Pulling into the parking lot, Alex drove around the building, looking for a good place to park. Most of the windows were blacked out. The only area that he felt comfortable parking was directly facing the cafe. The reason was that area had two double plated windows that were not blacked out. That way, he could sit in the cafe, read, sip his tea, and keep an eye on 'Spanky' The parking lot looked full.

"Jeez, doesn't anyone work anymore?" he said, laughing at the irony of that statement.

Just as he made that comment, a car backed out of a spot. By some miracle, it was the BEST spot, directly in front of the cafe.

"Finally, some good luck is coming my way!" he said pulling into the spot carefully.

After parking the car, Alex walked around the entire car, to ensure that everything was A-OK with his beloved 'Spanky'. He began walking to the entrance, when he realized that he forgot to lock it. He pulled the key chain out of his pocket, hit the automatic lock twice, making sure he heard the beep, and was on his way.

8

He walked directly to the cafe. The place was packed. As he waited in line for his tea, he surveyed the area for any open tables. None. What killed him the most about the situation was that most of them never bought anything. They used the cafe as a library. He saw one older gentleman reading a New York Times. Barnes & Noble doesn't even sell the paper.

'At least buy a beverage, you cheap fuck,' Alex thought to himself. 'No wonder why all of the places he liked to frequent were going out of business. 'They buy what they want online, and come here to read it!'

About to give up, he spotted one elderly woman sitting and talking with her friend at what first appeared to be one long table. Upon closer examination, Alex realized that they had pushed two smaller tables together. One was sitting at one table, while her friend listened intently from the second table.

He paid for his tea, and grabbed the latest issue of his favorite magazine 'Rue Morgue' off the magazine rack up front. He then walked to the tables where the two women were still deep in conversation. Without saying a word, he dropped the hot tea on the table, making both women jump.

Trying his best not to sound sarcastic, but failing miserably, Alex said, "Oh, excuse me. I didn't mean to startle you. It's just that there are no seats available, and you seem to be taking two tables. Do you mind moving over so I can sit here and read some of this fine literature?"

He then dropped the magazine on the table, eliciting the response he knew, and hoped he would get. The two elderly woman stared at the cover, which had someone known as 'The Tall Man' holding a giant sphere with blood on it. The headline read: This Issue Has Balls.

One of the women sighed, not quite hiding her disgust, and said,"Come on, Beverly. Let's go to Panera Bread across the street. I'm hungry."

Alex didn't believe they were hungry, but more importantly, he didn't care. He now had both tables all to himself. He took his jacket off, placed it on the backrest, sat down, spread his legs all the way out, and let out a contented "Ahhhh."

Finally, the day was getting better.

9

Directly across from him he heard some negative murmuring. He looked up to see two 20 something's staring at him. They both had the same slicked-back, black hair, along with the not quite grown in mustache. What made it even more amusing to Alex was that both were wearing the same dark blue, with white stripes running down both sleeves windbreaker. Alex did his best not to laugh. Instead of looking like a tough street gang, which he assumed was their intention, they looked more like a boy band reject. He smirked as he came up with their gang name: No Direction. The assumed leader looked at Alex and said,"Hey, you gotta problem?" Alex didn't want any trouble. He looked away, as he continued sipping his tea.

The leader of this future boy band continued. "That's right. I'm talking to you. Don't you dumb rich kids know the meaning of the word respect?" Alex was never one to back away from a fight, but after today's earlier debacle, he was in no mood to spend the afternoon in a holding cell with these clowns. He didn't give in to their taunting. Instead, he got up from his chair, pushed the chair back in, straightened out his jacket on the backrest, and walked to the bathroom. The bathroom was at the other end of the store. He hoped by the time he came back, these low-rent Abbott and Costello's would be long gone.

Alex stepped up to the urinal, letting out a long, powerful piss.

'Coffee, tea, and water is a horrible combination with the water pills he took to lower his blood pressure', he thought to himself. Walking back to the cafe, Alex took his phone from his back pocket. Checking his Facebook posts while walking almost caused several collisions, along with a few passive aggressive remarks from some of the people he almost collided with. He laughed it off, as he put his phone back in his pocket. He reached into his front pocket to grab his keys. He felt nothing. A small twinge of panic struck. He felt around in his other pockets. Nothing. Alex went into full panic mode when he realized that he must have left his keys in his jacket, which was hanging on the backrest in the cafe. He was still at the other end of the store. He broke into a full sprint. Several kids and adults wisely moved out of his way. He made it back to the cafe. He was relieved to see that his jacket was still there. His heart began to stop racing. He took a deep breath, and reached into his front left pocket. NOTHING! Back into panic mode. He ripped his jacket off the chair, searching every pocket. Still nothing. Alex looked up to see where the '2 Amigos were sitting. The table was empty. He frantically scanned from left to right, back to front. They were nowhere in sight. He walked over to the cashier that served him his tea. Maybe she had some answers. While looking over the counter to see where she was, a distraction from outside grabbed his attention. Looking out the window, Alex saw the hoodlums surrounding Spanky, laughing away. "FUUUUCK!" Alex screamed at the top of his lungs. Everyone in the cafe gave him dirty looks, along with a couple of, "SHHHH's", but he didn't care, and had no time to explain. He ran to the huge plate glass window, and began pounding on it. They looked inside, and began to laugh even harder. The leader of this 'gang' jiggled the keys in one hand, and gave Alex the finger with his other. He hit the remote, unlocking the car.

"Shit!" yelled Alex, as he began running for the entrance. He ran out the door, and around the side where Spanky was parked. It was too late. He ran after the trail of exhaust fumes, as the two laughed. The driver had the window down. He began waving his middle finger high in the air, as the two continued laughing hysterically. Without even stopping to look for traffic, the car screeched out onto the road. Alex ran to the end of the lot, breathing heavily. The car became a distant blur, as he stood hunched over, trying to catch his breath.

10

"Come on Tony. Go faster!" said the passenger, excited to be riding in their new car.

"Calm the fuck down. We don't need the PoPo pulling us over."

"Yeah, you're right."

"I'm always right, " said Tony, as he looked at his eager passenger with a sinister grin.

He pressed harder on the gas pedal, increasing the speed.

"Hell yeah! Now that's more like it."

They saw a car up ahead. Tony tapped the brakes. All he got was air. He pressed on the brakes harder. The car kept moving.

Tony was usually too cool to show any type of fear in front of his friends. This was different. He could feel his heart racing, and beads of sweat began forming on his forehead, as he continued down the road. His friend Vinnie sat in the passenger seat, laughing and screaming with joy, not realizing what was happening. He looked over at Tony, who was now pumping the brakes furiously with both feet.

"What the fu.." were the last three words spoken as Spanky slammed into the car in front of it. Tony turned the wheel, propelling it into a tailspin. It spun out of control, smashing into the guardrail. Both Tony and Vinnie were not wearing their seatbelts.

They were too 'cool' for that. Tony went flyng through the windshield. His decapitated head rolled until it hit a tree, lying there with his eyes and mouth left wide open, like that of a terror-stricken mummified pharaoh. Vinnie's body made it halfway through the windshield. His dead body lay there, with shards of glass on his face and body. His right eyeball was out of its socket, hanging flimsily by a tendon. The car that was hit was now pulled over to the side of the road where the driver was breathing convulsively. Not because of any serious injuries, more from fear and panic.

Alex had used his phone to call the police. He now heard sirens heading in the direction that his car was headed.

"Great. Now I can get Spanky back and enjoy my day!"

11

Back at the garage, Paul was working underneath a car. He stopped working when the cd he had playing ended. He lifted himself up and went to a case holding his favorite cd's.

"Ahh, now this is my all-time favorite!" exclaimed Paul as he put on AC/DC's 1979 classic, 'Highway To Hell'.

Paul began playing air guitar to Angus Young's opening riffs of the title track. He inadvertently knocked something off the shelf while doing that. He bent down to pick it up. It was a brake pad for a 2008 Red Corvette that should have been installed earlier. He picked it up, staring at it with a huge grin. Flashbacking to the remark that Alex made earlier about living down South because it will be warmer for him, Paul let out a sinister laugh, as he said, "Don't worry Alex. It's going to be real warm where you are going!"

He began laughing hysterically, as Bon Scott sang about taking a road trip on the 'Highway To Hell'.

THE END

THE LINCOLN
HOUSE MASSACRE

The doorbell rang at Joel Gianni's condo. Joel was renting a two-story condo, complete with two upstairs bedrooms, and a bathroom. The downstairs consisted of the living room and the kitchen. He was upstairs getting changed when the doorbell rang again.

"I'll be right there," he yelled.

The doorbell rang again. The person ringing the doorbell became impatient. The screen door opened, followed by four heavy knocks on the white oak door.

"Jesus Christ, I said I'll be right there," Joel said, now slightly agitated, as he walked quickly downstairs to the front door.

Joel opened the door. His 17-year-old cousin Jason stood with his fist raised, ready to strike the door again.

If you keep this up, you're going to lose the title of being my favorite cousin," Joel said mockingly.

Joel was 25 years old with short brownish hair, which curled up in the back if he neglected to cut it after a few weeks. He was thin, except for a small paunch that was beginning to develop. His friends joked that his two unusually skinny legs looked like two toothpicks attempting to carry a watermelon. He did his best to stay in shape, but found that his favorite activity after working 55-60 hours per week as a manager at Staples had become knocking back a few Sam Adams while falling asleep watching his favorite horror movies.

"I can't lose that title," shot back Jason. "I'm your only cousin."

Jason was a junior in high school. He was tall and gangly for his age. Most people would assume that he should be a great basketball player, but he had no interest in sports, and moved much too awkwardly to become a star player. With his short brown hair, most thought that Joel and Jason were brothers. Jason idolized everything Joel did, and Joel didn't mind him hanging around. They both had similar interests; their biggest being the Paranormal. They both loved anything and everything to do with ghosts, spirits and poltergeists. They have always wanted to see a ghost. Jason would stay over at Joel's condo most weekends, where the two of them would walk deep in the woods to the local cemetery, armed only with a flashlight and a camera. In the past, they would use disposable cameras, blindly taking as many pictures as they can, hoping for the best. Excitedly, they would rush down to the photo lab in Walmart the following morning to have their pictures developed. Most of the time they got nothing. On that rare occasion when something would appear, like a blurry light, Joel would joke that the developer was eating glazed donuts at the time. They were much happier now, snapping 25-30 pictures a minute on their I-Phone. Now they could instantly see what they took a picture of, deleting most of them as they went along. The occasional orb would appear. While Jason was excited, Joel yawned and said, "It's most likely a reflection."

"How could it be a reflection?" Jason would always ask. "We never use a flash."

Joel thought for a second, never really giving a good answer, but always denying the validity of it. He was more of a skeptical believer. He believed in the Paranormal, and the After-Life, but knew that most of the stories he read or heard on Ghost Tours were either embellished, or completely made up for entertainment value.

"Why are you here so early?" Joel asked, looking at the time on his phone. "The Ghost Tour begins at 8pm. It's only 5:30pm.

"I know," said Jason. "I just couldn't sit at the house anymore. I'm too excited."

"Well, make yourself comfortable. I just got home from work."

"Thanks."

Jason walked to the fridge, grabbed a water, walked into the living room, plopping himself on the couch. You're so lucky, "Jason yelled as Joel began walking upstairs to his bedroom.

Joel stopped at the top step, yelling downstairs to his younger cousin. "You call working 60+ hours a week at Staples fun?"

"Sure, as hell beats going to school every day."

Joel thought for a second, shrugged his shoulders, and said, "Yeah, I guess you have a point. I'll be down in a second."

Jason turned on the tv feeling like a King, with the remote in one hand, and his water in the other.

"Ahhh. Now this is the life!!!"

He began flipping through the channels, becoming more frustrated with each flip.

"Reality show. Cooking show. Antique show. Television has become so bad, I would settle for a healthy dose of 'You Are Not The Father' on Maury Povich. You know it's a sad state of affairs when I begin to miss Jerry Springer."

Laughing to himself, Jason began chanting, 'JERRY! JERRY! JERRY!'

"What the hell is happening down here?" asked Joel, as he walked downstairs into the living room.

"Don't make me call Steve Wilkos to come kick your ass!" he said jokingly.

That Mr. Clean wannabe couldn't even wipe his ass, let alone kick mine," shot back Jason.

Joel opened his mouth for a comeback, but began laughing.

"That was funny," was his only retort.

"Forget this shit they call television now. I just bought something that I know you'll love."

Joel picked up a bag that was lying on the floor, pulling out a DVD boxed set. He began unwrapping it, and said, "You gotta see this!"

"What is it?" asked Jason impatiently.

There you go again. Don't you know that Patience is a Virtue. Good things come to those who wait."

"Yeah, yeah, yeah," said Jason, waving his hand dismissively. "Put it in a Hallmark Card."

"Here you go, you sarcastic bastard," said Joel, as grabbed the 3 DVD's, throwing the empty box at Jason.

Jason missed the catch, dropping the box on the floor.

"Hmmm," he said picking up the box and reading it. "Penn and Teller's Bullshit. I like it already."

Penn and Teller were the cousin's favorite magicians. What they loved best about the duo was their lack of taking anything seriously, while taking everything seriously. Their entire act consisted of demonstrating to the audience how a trick was done. The genius was that they performed it so fast and proficiently, that not only could you not see how it was done, but you became even more confused, adding to the fun. They loved the fact that there was no phony stage show, or dramatic flair, like that pompous asshole David Copperfield.

"What's this? They have a new show now?"

"Yeah," answered Joel, as he inserted the disc. "It's called 'Bullshit. They debunk pretty much everything. This particular disc is my favorite. I have a strong feeling that it will be yours as well."

Jason began reading the main menu that listed every episode. Two caught his eye immediately: 'Talking to the Dead' and 'Ouija Boards'.

"Put on the episode about the Ouija Boards. The first thing they should debunk is the pronunciation. It's not OUIJEE, it's OUIJA with an 'A'!"

"Wow!" exclaimed Joel. "You are like the Paranormal's Andy Rooney."

"Who the hell is that?"

Joel began his impression of the cantankerous host: "You know what I hate....."

He could clearly see that his younger cousin didn't have a clue who this Curmudgeon of CBS was.

"Never mind. Let's watch some 'Bullshit'."

Jason and Joel became transfixed to the television as Penn Fraser Jillette and Raymond Joseph Teller began debunking all that had to do pertaining to Ouija Boards. First on the list was the pronunciation.

"See, I told you," said Jason proudly.

"Shh. I can't hear," shot back Joel.

The episode showed people asking the board questions. The board seemed to work perfectly fine. They were asked to stop, put on a blindfold, and continue asking the board questions. Unbeknownst to the two participants, the board was turned a complete 180. They asked the first question. The planchette automatically went to where the YES and NO should have been, proving that it was moved subconsciously by the two players.

Next up was the episode entitled, 'Talking to the Dead'. Both Jason and Joel remembered watching 'Crossing Over with John Edwards' several years ago. Penn and Teller began to prove that he and many other self-professed mediums were easily able to manipulate information out of their 'victims'. In most cases, the bereaved parent, son or daughter wanted desperately to hear from the dearly departed. The medium exploited that fact simply by saying, "I see a woman."

The person would blurt out, "Is it my mother?'

A sly smile would show on the medium's face, knowing that they had them exactly where they wanted. He or she would coax more information out of the person, and the message would always be the same: 'They said that they love you, and it's time to move on.' This was followed with tears. To prove their point, Penn and Teller brought in a random guy off the street to try this technique to the unsuspecting crowd. He had everyone crying hysterically by the end, thinking they were speaking with their loved ones.

Joel and Jason were loving this. They began making jokes throughout the episode, each attempting to be more sarcastic than the other. Without any warning, the lamp turned on. Both looked at each other with confusion. This was followed with nervous laughter by both.

"Was that you?" asked Joel.

"How the hell could it be me? I'm nowhere near the lamp!"

Humming 'The Twilight Zone' theme music, Jason laughed, and said, "It must be the dead. They are ready to talk!"

"Good! At least I will finally have someone here to have an interesting conversation with."

"I hope you at least make them pay rent," said Jason, nervously laughing.

The episode finished. Joel walked over to the television to put away the DVD.

"Come on, let's go to the Ghost Tour early. Maybe we can bring home my new guest a friend."

2

Joel used the key fob to unlock his car doors. Jason opened up the passenger side, and got in. Joel started the car, plugging in the address for the Ghost Tour on his phone, which was now being used as a GPS.

"Hey. Where is this place, anyway?" asked Jason.

It's about a half hour drive into Coventry. Once we get there, we take a bus, or a small van with our group to a dirt road fittingly known as Paranormal Parkway. According to the legend, if you tend to believe any of this, a small group of people were out sailing one summer night. A storm hit, washing them up on a small island."

"Don't tell me," interrupted Jason. "It was a 3-hour tour. Did the Professor have enough coconuts to create electricity for the entire group to live for the next 30 years?"

Somewhat irked by Jason's sarcasm, but also in a way admiring his knowledge of Classic Television, he said in an equally sarcastic manner, "Alright, I won't tell you that, or anything else, unless you shut the fuck up!"

Jason, knowing that even though there might be a hint of truth to that comment, but not enough to really anger Joel, shot back with, "Don't make me conjure up some spirits to do my dirty work for me."

Joel, knowing all too well that Jason will start a joke,

and run it into the ground if you let him, decided to continue with his story.

"The piece of land that this group of people washed up on was perfect to start a small town. There was plenty of water, plentiful wildlife for good eating, and acres and acres of land to build. Once the weather cleared, they went back out on the boat to gather family members, friends, and their belongings. It became a thriving town for more than 15 years before tragedy struck. "

Joel looked at the digital clock on his dashboard and said, "Ahh, look at the time. Story hour is over."

"Aww, come on. Don't keep a brother waiting."

"I won't keep a brother, or cousin waiting. I'm sure the entire history and more embellished facts of 'Paranormal Parkway' will be told in all its glory tonight."

3

What do you mean by embellished?" asked Jason. "I thought you were a believer of everything Paranormal."

"That I am, but as I mentioned in the past, I am what is known as a Skeptical Believer. I know that there is definitely something out there, BUT I also know that there are plenty of scammers out there trying to make a quick buck with a couple of scary stories. I'll make a bet with you."

"Ok, I'm in," said Jason.

"I'll bet you $20..."

"I'm definitely in!"

"Let me tell you what the bet is before you go off giving me your last $20."

Jason began to speak, but Joel put his hand out, as if to say, 'be quiet for a second', and continued speaking.

"I'll bet you $20 that this Ghost Tour features a story where a husband goes off to war, never to return. The wife continues to haunt the house, pining away for her deceased husband."

"What makes you say that?"

"Every Ghost Tour that I have been on, and I have been on a lot, feature all of the same stories. They just use different names."

Jason thought about that for a second. He hesitated before saying, "Alright. I'll do it. $20 that they don't use that story."

"What's the matter? You don't seem as confident as you were 5 minutes ago."
"Um, I'm confident that I will be $20 richer by the time this tour is over!"
"We shall see," said Joel. "We shall see."

4

10 minutes later, Joel pulled into a parking lot, where roughly 15-20 people were outside. Some were smoking, others were talking. As Joel parked the car, and the two got out, they could feel the nervous excitement emanating from the group.

"Hey. Could you unlock the door? I forgot my hoodie," said Jason.

"Oh, I forgot my hoodie. It's so cold outside. How will I ever survive?" mocked Joel.

It's still much more masculine than being caught with a 'Carpenter's Greatest Hit's' in my car."

"Hey! I told you that was my girlfriends," said Joel, now laughing. "Besides, at least I have a car to keep a CD in."

"Yeah, you got me there, but tonight I put my first down payment of $20 on my future Corvette, courtesy of my favorite cousin."

As Jason began putting his 'Clockwork Orange' hoodie over his head, the door to a small mini-bus that was parked in the lot opened.

5

A short, portly man walked off of the bus. He had brownish-reddish hair, with a severe case of horseshoe baldness. His horrible comb over wasn't fooling anyone. He was wearing a black t-shirt that featured on the front a long tunnel reaching down into a fiery pit, with a young man screaming in the flames. The shirt read: 'GATEWAY TO HELL GHOST TOURS'. This shirt would have been a XXXL on anyone else, but it wore more like a cut-off tee over his extended belly.

"Hey, I think the 'Gateway to Hell' for this guy is the tunnel leading to his stomach," whispered Jason.

"Hello everyone. My name is Dan. I will be your Spirit Guide for tonight."

Several people said, "HI Dan."

"What the hell is this? A Ghost Tour, or an AA Meeting?" Joel asked, laughing quietly to Jason.

"So, who would love to see a ghost?" Dan asked the crowd.

Jason, Joel and several others raised their hands.

Dan laughed and said, "You say that now. Let's see if you feel the same way later tonight as the spirits begin to appear."

Joel laughed, and said a bit louder than he expected, "It looks like the only spirits good ol' Dan has seen reside in an empty liquor bottle."

Several people behind Joel began to laugh.

"What's so funny?" asked Dan.

Everyone became quiet. Oblivious, Dan continued speaking.

"Ok, everyone on the bus. First stop: PARANORMAL PARKWAY. Let's hope the dead take mercy on you tonight."

Everyone got on the bus in an orderly fashion. Once everyone was situated, and the bus driver began driving, Dan asked, "So, how many people believe in ghosts?"

To no one's surprise, everyone's hand was in the air. Dan, realizing the ignorance of his question, said, "Yeah, that's about right. You wouldn't be here if you didn't believe."

The bus stopped in front of an old, run-down house. It was white with black shutters. The paint was chipping away in several areas, and it appeared that the shutters would fall off with the next heavy wind. Everyone began looking out of the window with curiosity. The people on the other side of the bus, stood up, walked over to the other side, crouching so they could also see out of the window. Some began taking pictures with their cellphones.

Dan began speaking. "Does anyone know what this house is?"

A middle-aged man wearing a Halloween movie t-shirt shouted out, "It's the Lincoln House."

Dan smiled, and said, "Yes. That's correct. Someone has done their homework. Now, does anyone know the story of the dreaded Lincoln House?"

The same man answered,"2 Murder's- 1 Suicide."

"Give that man a prize!" beamed Dan.

He continued. "The year was 1967. I remember because my parents had a house not far from here. I was only 5, and a hell of alot skinnier," he laughed, "But I remember it like it was yesterday. Herbert and Lillian Lincoln lived here with their two children. The entire town loved them. Not a bad word to say about the entire lot. Anyway, one day out of the blue, the entire family disappeared. Not a word from anyone. It didn't seem odd at first. Herbert had asked for some time off from the factory, while Lillian stayed home to take care of her two boys, Billy and David. If my memory serves me correctly, Billy was 12, and David was 10. Everyone at first just assumed that the family had taken a vacation. They always mentioned wanting to take a trip to visit Herbert's parents in Texas. Three weeks went by. Herbert was due back at work. He always arrived early to start work at 7am on the dot. By 11:30am, he still hadn't shown up. In the seven years that he worked at the factory, he was late once, and that was only because someone rear-ended him at a red light. The foreman became concerned. He tried his cell. No answer. He attempted to call the house phone. He let it ring 8 times, hung up, and let it ring another 8 times. No answer. Concerned that something was seriously wrong, he dialed 9-1-1. I hope that everyone here has a strong stomach, because what I am about to tell you is most likely the grossest, the sickest, and the most grotesque thing imaginable. People from past tours still e-mail me regarding the nightmares they still have due to this Tale of Terror. I've been telling this same story for years now, and it still makes me so sick that I make sure that I don't eat anything after 9am the day of the tour."

Jason elbowed Joel in the ribs as they sat together on the bus.

"If that's true," he whispered to his cousin, "he is the equivalent of a Culinary Marine: 'I eat more before 9am, than most people do all day!'"

A small chuckle from Joel as he let Dan continue his Ghastly Tale From Beyond.

"Two police cars pull up to 107 County Road approximately 5 minutes later. The first thing the police took notice of was the rancid odor emanating from the property. As you can see, just like it is now, this house is in the middle of nowhere. The next closest is 3 miles down the road. The two police officers hesitantly continue towards the door. The closer they were to the door, the stronger the odor became. They rang the doorbell, but of course there wasn't an answer. Officer # 1 opened up the screen door, and began pounding his fist on the inside wooden door.

Joel looked to Jason and whispered, "Sound like anyone you might know?"

Jason knew this was a slight dig at his impatience waiting for Joel to answer his door. He shrugged his shoulders and smiled.

Dan continued. "As Officer # 1 was ponding on the door, Officer # 2 began walking around the house, shining his flashlight to the left and right, looking for any clues. He searched the side, now making his way to the back. Nothing appeared suspicious, or out of the ordinary, until he reached the other side of the house. A large window that looked into the living room was covered in black. Curiosity overtook him, and he began running his hand up and down the large window. The blackness covered the window from the inside. He tapped the window with his right hand. The blackness began to move. The officer jumped back in surprise. The surprise turned into utter disgust when he realized the reason the blackness was moving was because it had wings. He pressed his face into the window. Thousands of flies began moving. He felt the food he ate earlier moving upwards, as his stomach began to turn. Officer # 1 gave up on the front door, and walked over to see what his fellow officer had found.

"Let's call for back-up," said Officer # 2.

"Officer # 1 replied, "Really? What are we going to report? An abundance of flies? The chief will send over a fly swatter, along with a box to put our balls in! Come on. We're going in."

Reluctantly, Officer # 2 agreed. They went back to the front door. Even though they both knew it was locked, Officer # 1 turned the door handle to open it. Officer # 1 said, "Stand back," and began kicking the door with his left leg. It took three attempts, and numerous uses of the word fuck, before he was able to kick the door in. As they walked in, they were immediately hit with the stench of death. Flies were everywhere. The officers began swatting them away from their faces in disgust. Officer # 2 bent over and began retching. A bit of mucus came up, but mostly it was a severe case of the dry heaves. As they walked deeper into the house, the stench became much worse. Both officers covered their noses using their sleeve. They followed the odor to a closed door. One looked to the other, as if asking for permission to open it up. The other officer nodded. Slowly, the door was opened, both afraid of what they would find. The other side of the door contained the family room, or den. In the middle of the floor, lay 2 young boys', minus their heads, thanks to a shotgun blast. Both bodies appeared to be repeatedly stabbed, with large cuts to the abdomen, arms, legs and back. This room was also covered with flies. Upon closer examination, both had large, brownish worms writhing in an on their bodies. Officer # 1 turned the body over with his foot. A maggot slimed his way out of the boy's ear. The contents of his breakfast spewed out of his mouth, and onto the floor. The maggots and flies were in their glory. Officer # 1 had to leave the room before he also became sick. He turned down the hall, entering the bedroom. On the bed, sprawled out, completely naked with a big hole in her chest, was the once beautiful Lillian Lincoln. She also had large stab wounds on her chest, face, legs and arms. Her long, blackish hair was now crimson, covered in blood. The officer stepped closer to the bed. Maggots were now feasting on this decomposing body. Before he had a chance to warn his fellow officer to stay clear, he walked in asking, "Did you find anything?"

No words needed to be spoken as they both stared at the decomposing piece of flesh. Officer # 2 patted his friend on the shoulder to get his attention. He stood there staring, as if in shock. He may have been on the force for 15 years, and THOUGHT he had seen it all, but he never encountered anything like this. He stood transfixed over the body of Lillian Lincoln. He felt the tap again. He pushed it away. Officer #2 used both hands to grab him by the shoulders, and turn him around so that they were now facing each other. Officer # 1 finally snapped back to reality. The second Officer # 2 pointed to the corner of the bedroom. Dead, and kneeling with his left hand resting on his chin, was Herbert Lincoln.

"Hey, was Herbert doing his best 'Thinker Portrait' impression?" asked Jason sarcastically.

That got some laughs, but mostly jeers, from the group that was listening intently to every word.

Dan, who must have heard that joke at least a million times on the tour, didn't miss a beat.

"The only thinking that was going on in his head was cold-blooded murder. A shotgun lay by his side. Both officers were amazed that the body could stay in that position for so long without falling over. Herbert had no apparent gun or stab wounds. That didn't stop the flies and maggots from discovering a fresh kill. Officer # 2 began examining the body, looking for the cause of death. Putting on his gloves, so not to tamper with the evidence, he grabbed Herbert's left arm. A severe case of rigor mortis had sunk in. The arm snapped in half, with the officer holding half of the arm in his hand. Whatever was left in his stomach, was now all over the floor, and some covering Herbert. He threw the arm on the floor. Later, an autopsy confirmed that after he killed his entire family with a large kitchen knife, and a shotgun, he went into the bedroom, knelt on the floor and overdosed on heroin. The spirits of Lillian, Billy and David have been seen in this area by many reputable people. Billy and David are known for their pranks and their playfulness. Herbert has never officially been seen, but some people have felt a dark presence, which we assume must be him. Lillian, on the other hand, has been known to throw things, and cause physical harm to those that have encountered her. My guess is that Billy and David were too young to fully comprehend what happened. Lillian does understand, and has become a malevolent spirit. I highly recommend that if you want to take pictures, please do it from the safety of the bus. You don't want to risk the chance of bringing back something with you."

That caused several gasps from the group. Joel and Jason were loving every second of this.

"How do you know so many intimate details regarding this? It sounds like you were there," said Joel arrogantly, hoping to prove to everyone that the story was highly embellished for the tour.

Again, Dan immediately had an answer.

"All you have to do is read the police report, like I did. It's all in there."

"Alright. If that's the case, then why did you make the 2 officers characters from a Dr. Seuss story, Thing One, and Thing Two?"

"The reason I did that," said Dan, now becoming irritated," was because the 2 officers were so traumatized by the events that they want nothing to do with that case. I was asked by their attorneys to keep their names confidential."

Jason looked at him and smiled. "Nice try, cuz."

"Any other questions?

No one said a word.

"Alright, if there are no questions, and everyone was able to take a picture or two, let's move on."

The tour continued, moving from one location to the next, each with a fascinating and scary story of hostile spirits and eerie happenings. The tour was coming to an end when Jason said, "Are you giving me that $20 in cash or check?"

Joel sighed, reaching into his back pocket to retrieve his wallet. He took out a $20 bill, and was about to hand it over in defeat when Dan said, "Alright Ladies and Gentlemen. We have one final stop. The bus came to a halt, and Dan began his next narration. "See how old this house looks? It appears that way for a reason. It was built back in 1772 for Mary and Todd Fitzgerald. The Revolutionary War was to begin 3 years later. Poor Todd went away to fight for his country, never to return. Distraught Mary waited and waited for the love of her life to return. She died heartbroken, waiting for him. Many say that she is still here waiting. Her spirit has been seen many times, crying, with tears flowing down her beautiful face."

Joel looked at Jason and laughed. "Looks like that Corvette will have to wait!"

"Damn!" exclaimed Jason. "I was so close."

Dan opened the door to the bus, allowing everyone to get out and take pictures. Obviously, he wasn't as worried about sad, lonely Mary coming back home with any of the group, like he was with Lillian.

6

Jason and Joel, never taking anything seriously, took selfies of themselves appearing dead in some, and looking mock terrified in others. Some of the guests walked by them, giving the two dirty looks. One woman stopped taking pictures, and began watching the two making a mockery of the Paranormal.

"I hope you're having fun now," she blurted out. "Because if I bring anything back with me, I'll sue you!"

The two boys were stunned at first, staring at the woman incredulously. Joel broke the silence.

"Good luck with that lady. I'm sure Trantolo and Trantolo will jump all over that!"

Joel and Jason broke into laughter. The woman walked away into the darkness, back to the group, shaking her head. Joel and Jason continued taking more selfies, along with pictures of the house, and the surrounding area, hoping to catch some sign of the Afterlife. If not, at least they were going home with some funny Facebook and Instagram posts. The bus started. Looking around, they realized that they were the only two left outside.

"Shit! Wait for us!" screamed Jason, still laughing as they ran back to the bus.

Dan began a head count after everyone had boarded.

"I hope everyone had a great time," he said. If you find out later that you took some great pictures of the Paranormal, please share it on my Facebook page, or e-mail me at dan the man @ gateway to hell.

"Why wait until later? Let's see what we have now," said Joel scanning the pictures on his I-Phone. He was swiping fast and furious as Jason looked on.

"Nothing. Nothing. Still nothing. Wait. What's that? Ah, forget it. Still nothing," Joel said disgustedly, swiping through the many pictures that were taken.

"Go to the pictures of the Lincoln House," said Jason.

Joel continued swiping, no longer looking at the pictures, until he reached the Lincoln House.

"Here we go!!"

The first three pictures seemed normal. He was about to swipe again when Jason stopped him.

"Wait, what's that in the corner?" asked Jason.

"It's the window that was covered with flies back in the day," answered Joel.

"I know. What's that in the corner?"

"I don't see anything."

Jason sighed, and said, "Just give me the phone. I'll show you."

Jason grabbed the phone, zooming in and out on the bottom left hand corner of the window.

"I don't see anything," said Joel, sounding annoyed.

"Give me a second, Mr. Patience!"

"Touché!"

Jason continued zooming in and out and said, "Here you go!"

Handing the phone back to Joel, he asked, "Now do you see it?'

The couple behind them were now looking over their shoulders with curiosity.

Jason said, "Right here, Stevie Wonder!"

He pointed to what looked like 2 young boys smiling in the bottom left hand corner of the window. A dark mist seemed to envelop the two boys.

"Holy Shit! exclaimed Joel, now grabbing the attention of everyone on the bus, including Dan.

Dan walked over to the two boys asking, "Did you capture anything besides my attention?"

He was the only one laughing at his joke. Joel handed Dan his phone.

"I'm not sure. What do you think this is?"

Dan looked intently at the phone, putting it right up to his nose. Sighing, he took a pair of reader glasses that he had bought at Big Lots out of his back pocket, and put them on.

"Sorry. Without these, I am as blind as a bat."

He zoomed in, zoomed out, turned the phone sideways, upside down, and right back.

"Holy Shit is right! You have a picture, a pretty clear one at that, of the infamous Lincoln boys."

"What do you think about the dark mist covering, almost wrapping itself around the boys is?" asked Jason.

"What I think you have here boys, is a good old-fashioned family portrait. The dark mist is most likely the malevolent force that was once the beautiful and loving Lillian. It appears that she is attempting to pull them back into her world, whatever that may be. Please e-mail this to me. I need to put this on my site."

By now everyone began to get up to catch a glimpse of the picture. Dan realized that he was losing control of his group.

"Ok people. Sit back down. I'm sure once the bus stops, they will be more than happy to show you their picture."

Disappointed, everyone went back to their respective seats. Joel and Jason were too excited to think about anything else. They had been on many ghost tours, but this was the first time they had ever captured anything more than orb. The bus stopped back at the lot. Jason and Joel were the first to get off. They walked directly to the car, wanting to avoid everyone's questions. They succeeded.

7

On the trip back to Joel's condo, Jason said, "I have a great idea. Let's take out the Ouija Board to see if we can connect with any of our new 'friends'."

Joel looked at him reluctantly. "We both just watched Penn and Teller prove what a crock of shit that is."

"Au Contraire, my skeptical cousin. You and I both know that most of it is complete bullshit, but we also know that deep down some of it might be real."

"You do have a point," said Joel, hitting the gas, looking forward to this Night of Paranormal to continue.

The ride home was a blur to the two, as they excitedly went over the night's events, and the paranormal pictures taken of the infamous Lincoln family. Once inside the condo, Joel ran upstairs to grab the Ouija Board from his bedroom closet. Jason waited impatiently downstairs. Joel appeared at the top of the stairs holding the board high above his head.

"Got it! The best, and only good thing that Parker Brothers ever invented."

"Will you stop with the damn commercial, and get down here. I want to speak to the spirits."

"Alright, alright," said Joel, walking down the stairs. "Speaking of spirits, I have a 12-pack of Corona with our names on it."

"Aw, come on. That's pussy beer," said Jason.

"Pretty big talk for a 17-year-old!"

Joel put the board on the kitchen table, went to the fridge, grabbing two 'pussy beers'. With the cold brew now directly in front of him, Jason said, "Well, I guess I could slum it for one night."

Joel placed the board on the kitchen table, as Jason pulled his chair forward.

"Hey, where's the pointer? "Jason asked.

"Holding it in his hand, Joel condescendingly said, "OH, you mean the planchette?"

Mocking his cousin, Jason repeated in a high pitch sarcastic tone, "Yes, I mean the planchette."

"Why didn't you say so in the first place?" laughed Joel as he placed it on the board. "LET THE GAMES BEGIN!"

Joel placed 2 fingers on one side of the planchette, as Jason placed his two fingers on the other side.

Instantly, the planchette began moving in a circular motion. Jason and Joel looked at each other accusingly, as if to say, 'Is that you messing around, or is it really moving on its own?'

As if reading Joel's mind, Jason blurted out, "I'm not moving it!"

"Then I guess it's time to ask the first question," said Joel, taking a sip of his Corona. "Is there a spirit here in the room?"

"Wow! That's original," mocked Jason.

"Remember, Patience is a Virtue."

"Yeah, save it for a fortune cookie, Buddha!"

"Hey, we need to start slow. Trust me. Let me repeat the question. Is there a spirit....."

Joel was unable to finish his sentence as the planchette slid over to the word YES.

Jason took his hand off of the planchette to take a sip of beer.

"We can drink later. I don't want to interrupt the flow," scolded Joel.

Becoming irritated with his older cousin, but more excited to be playing with the Ouija, Jason said,"Ok, let me ask a question."

"Be my guest."

The planchette began circling as Jason began his question. "Alright, was this spirit mentioned on tonight's Paranormal Tour?"

The planchette slid over to the word YES. Joel asked the next question. "Are you a member of the Lincoln family?"

The planchette circled several times before settling on the word YES.

Jason blurted out, "Is this Billy or David?"

The planchette slid to the word NO. Excitement and nervous curiosity were intensifying as Joel asked the next question. "Are you the infamous Herbert?"

The planchette circled 4 times, settling on the word NO.

"Well, there is only one person left," said Jason. "Who are you?"

The planchette began circling the entire board, performing a figure 8. The boys couldn't stop it, even if they wanted to. It stopped, and began spelling a word. First a L, sliding to an I, then to L, circling once, resting once again on L, then an I, across the board to A, finally stopping at the letter N. In unison, the two boys yelled out, "LILLIAN!"

"Are you Lillian Lincoln?" asked Jason.

The planchette slid almost on its own to the word YES. As if on cue, a cool breeze blew through the kitchen window. Joel shivered, not quite sure if it was from the breeze, fear, or both.

"HOLY SHIT! exclaimed Jason. "We have our self a certified ghost."

Joel, once again being the skeptical believer, attempted to bring his cousin back to reality.

"Before we go on celebrating, let's make sure it's genuine."

Jason, now feeling disappointed, said, "And how in the hell do you expect to achieve that, Old Wise One?"

"Well, remember what Penn and Teller mentioned in their special?"

Jason interrupted him, knowing exactly where he was going with that.

"You are a genius," he said, flipping the board around.

"Exactly. Now that the board is turned 180, let's see if the planchette moves to where the YES and NO should be, not where it is."

Joel took a sip of his pussy beer, and asked the next question. "Is this really Lillian Lincoln?"

The planchette began circling, gaining speed, accelerating to several Figure 8's across the board. Jason and Joel looked at each other, amazed and astonished. The planchette began going where the word YES should have been, stopping for a second. The two cousins took their hands off the planchette. The planchette then slid to the other side of the board on its own where the word YES was now.

"FUCK ME!" said Jason, standing up from the table. Joel began laughing. "Sorry, cuz. You are NOT my type! Now sit back down. I thought the only pussy in here was the beer."

Still shaken, Jason gave a nervous laugh, and sat back down. Before resuming the game, he downed his Corona in one continuous swig. Wiping his mouth with his wrist, he said, "Let's do it!"

"Is this a Nike Commercial, or Paranormal Night with the Gianni's?"

Joel went to the refrigerator, grabbing two more beers. He sat down, and asked the next question. "Ok, if this is really Lillian Lincoln, then how were you murdered?"

The two watched in amazement as the planchette spelled out the words SHOT and STABBED.

"Next question," said Jason. "How were Billy and David murdered?"

The planchette began circling faster, as if possessed. The words SHOT and STABBED were once again spelled out. The kitchen light began to flicker. Drinking another beer, and feeling a bit looser, Joel joked, "Now you went and pissed the bitch off!"

Jason, being even more of a lightweight than his cousin, was now feeling a bit of the liquid courage. Sarcastically he said, "Well, I'm so sorry ma'am for disturbing your slumber. I know how hard it is trying to get some rest in the Afterlife!"

Joel, upping the sarcasm, asked,"Are you more like Casper the ghost, or that piece of shit in 'Poltergeist'?"

The planchette didn't move.

Jason cracked open another Corona and asked, "What's the matter? Herbert got your tongue?"

The planchette stayed in place.

"Ok, I can understand your reluctance answering these questions, but I have a question you can't refuse," said Joel, now doing his best Marlon Brando from 'The Godfather' impression. "Are you more like Glinda the Good Witch, or her sister, the Bitch from the West?"

The planchette suddenly sprang to life, surprising the two. It began circling the board all on its own. Jason and Joel watched, unable to move, as if paralyzed. The board began spelling out words. Moving at lightning speed, the two read as it spelled out the sentence: 'DON'T FUCK WITH ME'!

Jason, chugging the last of yet another beer, said, "Oh, yeah. We have a live one, and I use that term loosely!"

Whatever fear and apprehension Jason and Joel felt was now completely absent, as these two lightweight drinkers were now taking everything as a joke.

Joel laughed,"Alright. I promise not to fuck with you. Besides, you're not even my type."

Joel continued. "I have final question, and I promise to leave you alone. When will my favorite cousin Jason meet his untimely demise?"

"Hey! Fuck you!" said Jason laughing.

The planchette began moving again. It circled twice, and did one figure 8 around the board before spelling out the word TOMORROW.

8

Joel began laughing. "I guess we should go now, seeing that I have a funeral to plan."

Jason, still feeling good, and not taking it seriously, asked, "Let me make sure I read that correctly. Are you trying to tell me that I will be dead tomorrow?" The planchette slid to the word YES.

"Jason stood up, taking a large gulp of his beer. "Well, alright. I guess Party Time is Officially Over!"

Joel took his hand off of the planchette. Without any help, the planchette began circling. Before anyone had a chance to comprehend what was happening, the planchette raced off of the board on its own at lightning speed, sticking into the wall. The kitchen light began to flicker. Jason, a bit startled, but his liquid courage still strong, blurted out, "She'd make a great pitcher. Her fastball is phenomenal!"

Joel stood up, pulling the planchette out of the wall, and began examining the damage.

"What the fuck! My landlord is going to kill me!"

"You were warned, Joel. She said not to fuck with her!"

"Yeah, try telling my landlord that an angry dead bitch put a hole in the wall."

"Forget all about that for now. I say we go check out the house tonight. It's 10:30pm now. The Witching Hour is at 12am. The Devil's Hour is at 3am. I say we finish a couple more brewski's, and make our way to the Lincoln homestead."

Joel was angry, but too buzzed to think coherently. "Yeah, I think that's a great idea. Maybe I can collect some money from the dearly departed Lillian for the damage."

"If not that, the least you can do is ask for rent money, seeing that she is making herself very comfortable in your condo."

The anger subsided a bit, and Joel laughed. "Alright cuz. We have 6 beers left. Let's drink the spirits before going out to see some."

The two drank, talked and laughed until the final beer was finished. The clock on the stove read 11:15pm. Only 45 minutes left to the Witching Hour. Jason was upstairs using the bathroom. Joel called up to him. "Come on, man. We gotta go. Drain that peanut-sized bladder of yours, and let's get the hell out of here."

Jason finished, turned off the light, and began walking downstairs. "You know better than anyone that once you break water for the first time, it's ALL OVER!"

"You don't see me going every 2 minutes, do you?!"

"Well, excuse me, Mr. Man of Steel. Correction: Mr. Bladder of Steel!"

Jason let out a loud yawn.

"Oh, look at Mr. Lightweight," laughed Joel. "Does the little baby need a nap?"

Yawning again, Jason said, "No, of course not. Let's go."

The two began the drive back to Coventry. Jason moved around in the passenger seat, attempting to make himself comfortable. His eyes began getting heavier. Joel started to protest, but before he had a chance, Jason was fast asleep, his eyes fluttering at a maddening pace. Joel looked at his sleeping cousin and laughed. "Pussy beer, my ass!"

The ride went smoothly. There was hardly any traffic, and best of all, his WAZE app didn't detect any police. Joel was smart enough to park his car down the street from the dreaded Lincoln House, where it was obscured by trees.

"Wake up Sleeping Beauty."

Joel began to shake him. Jason groaned. Joel shook him again. "Wake up, Rip Van Winkle."

Jason, now agitated, said, "I'm up. I'm up."

"Sure, you are."

Jason stretched both his arms and legs as much as he was able to in the confined passenger seat. "Come on. Let's go." said Jason.

"Oh, now you're all gung-ho. Well, now it's time for my nap."

Jason, still a bit groggy, surprisingly didn't have any smart-ass comeback. He moved on to a different subject.

"I had the weirdest dream."

"Why was it weird? Were you cool and popular? Now that would be a weird dream."

Jason, still too groggy for Joel's sarcasm, said, "Besides the fact that I am ALREADY cool, and ALREADY popular, my dream was about Lillian Lincoln. You were in it as well. And just like in real life, you were an asshole."

"Oh, I have to hear this!"

Jason continued with his story. "I dreamed that Lillian was cheating on her husband. Good ole Herbert found out. As you can imagine, he wasn't the happiest camper. He ended up killing her, and the guy she was fucking."

Joel interrupted. "Is that where I come in. Did I fuck Lillian?"

Jason, finally beginning to wake up said, "No way. That wouldn't be a dream. It'd be a NIGHTMARE! Later on, a search party, which included you, went searching through the woods. We found the body wrapped in a net."

Joel interrupted again. "A net?"

"I know. I don't quite understand it either. Anyway, if you stop interrupting me, and let me finish the goddamned story, I can tell you."

Joel held up his arms as if surrendering.

"As I was saying, we found her in a net. You exclaimed to the search party, who were now visibly shaken, "What's wrong? Looks like everyone just got stung by a WHORE NET! Then I woke up."

"A whore net? That's hilarious," laughed Joel.

"Just goes to show you that even in dreams, you are a complete asshole!" laughed Jason.

Opening up the car door, Joel said, "Let's hope the whore net doesn't sting us tonight."

Jason opened his door, following Joel to the house., which was up the road from where they were parked. Making sure that they both had their phones on them, they were on their way. Now standing directly in front of the house, they observed all of the NO TRESPASSING and VIOLATOR'S WILL BE PROSECUTED signs, along with the yellow police tape covering the perimeter of the yard.

"A couple of signs can't stop us," said Joel, the two stepping over the tape.

Jason responded with a large yawn. Joel slapped him on the back. "What's the matter? Pussy beer wipe you out!"

Jason rubbed both eyes vigorously with his palms. "Never. Let's go find us some ghosts."

"Even though there isn't a neighbor within miles, let's keep it quiet," said Joel. "I'm sure Coventry's finest still patrol this area on a regular basis."

"No worries there," said Jason, letting out a big yawn. Before Joel had a chance to comment, Jason extended his arm, as if to say, 'Shut the fuck up!' The sky was clear, not a cloud in the sky. The moon was full, giving off a reddish-orange glow, making it easy to see without using their flashlight app on their phones.

Joel whispered,"Hey, there's the window that was completely covered with flies. Let's start there."

"I'm right behind you."

The two walked up to the window, pressing their faces into it. It was dark, but they could both make out the living room furniture in disarray. Dark stains covered the floor. Blood they both assumed. Joel took out his phone, snapping away pictures.

"Don't use the flash. All you get is our reflection, which is far scarier than any ghost," warned Jason.

"This isn't my first rodeo. I know how to take a great ghost picture," shot back Joel.

The two began snapping away. Jason stopped to examine his pictures.

"Hey, let's take as many pictures as we can now. We'll check for signs of life, or should I say afterlife, later," said Joel.

Jason nodded in agreement, and yawned. Joel just sighed, and began walking around the house. Jason followed, as the 2 spent the next 25 minutes snapping pictures of everything and anything.

"Come on, let's go inside," whispered Joel.

Yawning in response, Jason said, "Let's come back some other time. It's not that I'm afraid. I am just so damn tired, and I'm not afraid to admit it."

"Don't wimp out on me now, cuz. We're already here. Who knows the next time we'll make it here again."

"Ah, great move. The old peer pressure trick. I have to admit that I like your style. There's only one problem. You know that I NEVER succumb to peer pressure!"

"That's right," said Joel. "You don't. You only succumb to sleep. Should I take you home and tuck you in?"

Too tired for his sarcasm, Jason said, "Do what you want. I'll get an Uber."

Joel, now more determined than ever to walk throughout The Lincoln House, said,"Alright. Text me when you get back to my place."

Feeling tired and aggravated, Jason said, "Maybe I'll just go home."

"Do whatever the hell you want, but you and I both know that your parents will rip you a new asshole if they see you walking in the house like this!"

"Whatever," said Jason, waving his hand, dismissing Joel. It wouldn't be the first time I snuck in downstairs, and it most definitely won't be the last."

9

Joel didn't bother with a response. He instead began walking to the back, looking for an easy way to get into the house without getting hurt, and most importantly, without alerting the law.

Jason pulled out his phone, bringing up the Uber app.

"Ah! Here's one only 5 minutes away. Yes, Jose, you can be my driver."

The wind picked up again, rustling the leaves in the trees.

"I must be damn tired. The wind sounds like a woman screaming. I never get spooked. My imagination is running wild tonight."

Joel reached the back entrance, and stopped. He thought he heard a scream. He shivered from the cool breeze, gave a nervous laugh, and continued walking up the steps to the back door.

The wind blew again, this time a bit stronger, and feeling a bit cooler. Jason shivered, as he held the phone to check the time.

"12:48 in the morning," he said yawning.

A gust of wind picked up, the sound of a woman screaming becoming much louder. He turned to his right. Jason noticed a large mass of black mist swirling above the ground. He stared at it in both fear and awe as it picked up speed.

Before he had a chance to make a move, the black mist began swirling faster and faster, now coming directly at him. As it came closer, he could detect some features in the middle of the swirl. It was if a spotlight was beaming. He saw very clearly a woman with a dark complexion, long, flowing black hair, piercing blue eyes, wearing a white gown, flowing behind her. The scream became so loud that a window on the house cracked from the noise. "What the fu....?!" was his only response as the dark mist enveloped him. He was thrown backwards. In a state of shock, Jason stood up to dust himself off. He felt sharp pain up and down his arms. Both had deep scratches all over. He heard the scream again, this time from behind him. It all happened so fast that Jason didn't have time to do anything but watch as the dark mist featuring the woman with the white, flowing gown hit him from behind, throwing him 10 feet in the air. His head smacked the giant oak tree in the front yard. Dazed, confused, and in much pain, he still couldn't comprehend what was happening to him. Jason felt the back of his head with his right hand. It was warm. Looking at his hand using the moon as light, he noticed fresh blood. A bit shaken, but still attempting to maintain his sense of humor, he muttered, "hit! Now I know what Sonny Bono felt on his last day of skiing!"

He stood up, his right hand holding the back of his head. He staggered backwards, only stopping when he noticed that the ground he was standing on was extremely soft.

"What the hell is this, some kind of sinkhole?"

It only took several seconds for Jason to receive his answer. The scream started up again, as the black mist enveloped Jason one final time. The woman with the long black hair grew bigger and bigger, her mouth opening wider, so big that it was now blocking out the moon. She lunged forward, swallowing Jason whole. He fell backwards, the earth caving in as he fell to his death.

10

The wind and the deafening screams came to an abrupt halt. The only evidence of Jason being at The Lincoln House was his cellphone lying on the grass, which was thrown from his hand as he fell.

Joel had the screen door open, and was attempting to open the inside door. He stopped when he heard what sounded like a woman's angry scream for the 3rd time. The first two times he thought it was his over active imagination mixed with alcohol, and lack of sleep. Joel rolled his eyes, muttering, "What now?" He was walking to the front when he saw a pair of headlights. The car was moving very slowly in front of the house. It didn't stop completely, but continued down the road at a snail's pace. Joel continued to the front.

"What the hell is this?" he said, picking up a small black object on the front lawn. "SHIT!" he said upon closer examination. "Jason dropped his cellphone." He began running after the car, waving his hand with the cellphone frantically.

"Hey, dipshit. You forgot your damn phone! Hey! Hey!"

His pleas went unheard as he watched the Uber's taillights disappear, taking a left back into civilization.

"Looks like I won't be receiving a text tonight," said Joel, placing the cellphone in his back pocket.

Joel looked back up at the house, letting out a huge yawn. Looking at his cellphone for the time, he muttered,"1:15 in the morning. Maybe my pussy of a cousin has a point. I'll come back some other time. These 60-hour work weeks are killing me!"

That excuse always made him feel better about not following through with a plan. He walked down the street to his parked car, unlocking it with the FOB. The ride home was spent yawning, and turning the radio to a different station every few seconds, hoping to find a better song than the one he was listening to. The digital clock in his car read 2:04am, as he pulled into his condo parking lot.

"Jesus H Christ. Why am I so fucking tired?" he asked himself, yawning again.

He laughed at how it sounded. "Why would I ask Jesus, and what does the H stand for: HELP?!"

He laughed even harder, opening the door to his condo. Placing his and his cousin's cellphones on the kitchen table, he noticed DVD's and CD's strewn about the living room. The refrigerator was wide open.

"Holy Shit! Was I robbed?"

Worried that the intruder might still be inside, Joel slowly, and silently crept upstairs towards his bedroom. He peeked around the corner into his bedroom. NOTHING. He peered to the left checking the spare room and the bathroom. NOTHING.

Letting out a giant sigh of relief, he turned on his bedroom light. The bed was ransacked. The comforter was on the other side of the room, and the sheets were on the floor. The stereo was turned on. It was on Auxiliary, meaning no music was playing. Turning it off, he scanned the room to see if anything was missing. The clothes that he had left on the bed were now thrown on the floor. Shaking his head, he walked to the bathroom. The towels were on the floor, but everything else seemed to be in place. Feeling numb, he walked to the spare bedroom. Joel had his hand on the light switch, but stopped dead in his tracks at what he saw looking out the window. The blinds were taken off recently, and he never had the chance to replace them yet. He could see clear across the parking lot of the condo complex to the building directly across from him. A bright light was on in the other condo. Normally, something like this wouldn't even register with Joel, but this was not a normal night. He was known to many of his friends as Mr. Magoo; the clueless, yet lovable cartoon character. They always laughed that Joel could be walking around, happy as a clam, as chaos surrounded him. People could be getting shot, stabbed or set on fire, and he would be walking around without a care in the world. He wasn't exactly clueless, just self-absorbed. Tonight, was different. He stopped, staring intently at what he saw. A slender woman with long flowing black hair, wearing a white night gown was staring back at him.

It seemed to Joel that she was transparent, and floating. Looking through her, Joel could see his neighbors watching television. She looked at him with a sinister smile. His neighbor got up, went to the kitchen, and came back with a soda, resuming sitting on the couch, and watching tv. Obviously, they couldn't see or hear her. He stared back, paralyzed by fear. The woman with the long flowing black hair opened her mouth. A deafening, blood-curdling scream was released. Joel stood in place, transfixed at what he was witnessing. The windows began to shake.

"This is fucking nuts!" he said, finally snapping out of it. He ran down the stairs to grab his cellphone, ready to call the police. He picked his up first. DEAD. He threw it down, now trying Jason's phone. Also, dead.

"What the fuck?!"

The wailing became louder, his downstairs window violently shaking. Looking out the window, he could see the woman clearer than ever, mouth open wide, screaming. Only half-joking, not quite understanding why he would choose now to joke, said to himself, "Who the hell are you? Lillian Lincoln, coming back from the dead to claim another victim?"

As if answering his question, the kitchen lights began to flicker. The light switch was turned off. In that weird stage of still feeling drunk, with the hangover already beginning to kick in, not to mention fear and adrenaline coursing through his body, Joel yelled, "LEAVE ME THE FUCK ALONE, BITCH!"

11

Immediately, all of the lights in his condo flickered. Joel flipped the light switch in the kitchen on. The light bulb exploded. He used his forearm to shield his face and eyes from the flying glass. Without thinking, he turned the switch used to light the stairwell. The light bulb at the top of the stairs exploded. Feeling a combination of fear and anger, Joel felt compelled to look outside for the woman with the white gown. Joel grabbed his keys from the kitchen table.

"Fuck this! I'm going directly to the police station." Joel stepped outside, opened up his car door, and stopped.

"Where the hell do I think I am going?" he mused. "First of all, I am most likely legally drunk, and second of all, as much as I'd hate to admit it, I am guessing that this is the work of the late, great Lillian Lincoln. It might prove difficult to put her behind bars, and more importantly, it might prove more difficult to keep my drunk ass out of jail!"

Going back inside, he continued speaking out loud. "I'll take my chances with the Walking Dead over Deputy Dog anyday."

It was pitch black inside the condo. The only flashlight he had was the app on his phone, which was dead. Feeling tired and helpless, he made his way to the kitchen cabinet, where he kept his medication. Grabbing a large bottle, he shook it to ensure that he wasn't out. Hearing the pills rattle, he said, "Ahh, this is exactly what I need."

Joel emptied 5 Melatonin pills into his hand, promptly putting them in his mouth. They were chewable, so he didn't need any water.

"This will get me some much-needed sleep until I can drive to the authorities in the morning. Why do I suddenly feel like Teddy Kennedy on the night of Chappaquiddick?"

Not bothering to look for his usual nighttime attire, which consisted of sweatpants and a t-shirt, Joel plopped into bed. The melatonin, mixed with the beer, knocked him out almost immediately. He wasn't one to normally remember his dreams, but tonight was different. He felt a tug on his right leg. He shuffled a bit, groaned, turning over to his left side. He felt the tug again. His eyes still closed, he pulled his leg up to his chest, and let go a strong kick. Now he rolled onto his back, both legs fully stretched. He felt the tug again. This time he opened his eyes. Hovering over him was the woman he saw across the parking lot screaming in the window. She was transparent, the long, flowing black hair, and the white gown blowing, as if she was caught in a small breeze. Even though it was pitch back in the room, the woman was illuminated. She opened her mouth wide, baring her rotted teeth. Her breath smelled like Death. As she opened her mouth wider, she let out a deafening scream that seemed much louder, and scarier than earlier. Her eyes became a dark red, as if possessed by the Devil himself.

In a state of panic, Joel closed his eyes, hoping that when he reopened them, she would be gone. Unfortunately, when he opened them she was still hovering over him, her eyes becoming brighter, and her scream much louder. Not knowing what else to do, he pulled the comforter over his head, holding it tight. He closed his eyes even tighter. The scream continued, causing the windows to shake. In a Hail Mary, Joel ripped the comforter from over his head, and screamed, "GET THE FUCK OUT OF HERE, LILLIAN!!"

The screaming stopped. He opened his eyes, looking around his room. The lights were now on, and the digital clock on the nightstand was blinking 12:00. The woman was gone. Joel let out a nervous laugh. "Was that just a fucked-up dream?" he asked himself. 'If that was only a dream, it was the most realistic dream that I ever had,' he thought.

Joel got up, and went downstairs to check the phones. He saw the two on the kitchen table. Both had power. Grabbing his, he checked the time. "2:38. Damn. This has been one hell of a long night!" he said, walking back upstairs.

Joel corrected the time on his digital clock, set his alarm for 10am, and popped two more melatonin. Even with all of the adrenaline coursing through his body, it was still no match for five sleeping pills. The last thing Joel saw as he closed his eyes was the digital clock reading 2:47.

144

12

The alarm began going off, startling Joel. He sat up in his bed. Not only was the clock alarm going off, but so was the alarm on his phone. He could also hear Jason's alarm downstairs. Shutting off the clock, and his phone, he looked at the time, and muttered, "What the fuck?"

The time read 3:00am. The Devil's Hour. Feeling groggy and disoriented, Joel got up, and began walking downstairs to turn off the alarm on Jason's phone. The sound of two young boys laughing caused him to stop. It sounded like it was coming from the condo next door. The only problem was that the condo had been vacant for the last six months. Joel followed the noise upstairs to the bathroom, where the laughter became louder through the walls. He distinctly heard one boy say, "Come on, Billy. Let's play."

Joel stood up on the toilet, pressing his ear to the wall. He could hear rustling, as if the 2 young boys were running around the condo. "There you are. I found you. You're it!"

The laughing abruptly stopped, as the two boys began screaming," NO, DADDY, NO!!!"

The boy's pleas for help were drowned out by a deafening scream. It was so loud that the walls reverberated.

The force was so strong that it threw Joel off the toilet, his back smashing into the towel rack. The back of his head hit the wall with such strength, leaving a good-sized hole. He then fell forward, his mouth hitting the side of the bath tub. A loud crack was heard as his front teeth smashed in half; small pieces lying in the tub. Joel's body was slumped over the side of the tub, blood pouring from his mouth and the back of his head. A steady stream made its way to the drain, circling, then disappearing down the drain. He was completely knocked out. His body twitched several times, and then he lay still.

13

The digital clock read 7:30am. Joel began to waken. Every movement made him groan in pain. His eyes were closed, as his body became restless in the tub. More movement meant more groans. Still groggy, and not remembering what happened, he opened his eyes. Total darkness. Extreme fear instantly replaced the intense pain. He closed his eyes again, rubbing them with his palms. He opened them again to see darkness. He jumped up, rubbing his eyes even harder, hoping to bring his sight back. Joel grabbed the shower curtain in a panic, attempting to regain his footing. Placing his right leg over tub, he tripped, falling backwards into the tub, hitting his head against the wall. This caused him to see a white flash, then another, then a third. He opened his eyes, and was shocked and confused at what he now saw. He was in the Lincoln House. Confusion was taken over by terror as he looked to his right. Two young boys were sitting Indian style next to him, bobbing back and forth, laughing. Both had short dirty blonde hair, wearing tie-dyed shirts with bell bottoms. The clothes on both boys were covered with blood, but neither had a care in the world. Joel noticed what looked like multiple stab wounds on both. As if looking right through him, not at him, one of the boys said, "Would you like to play with me and David? Let's play hide n seek. You count."

The fear intensified as he realized that he was talking to the very dead Billy and David Lincoln. Opening his mouth as if to scream, he shut it when he saw that Jason was also on the room, on the other side of the Lincoln boys. Jason didn't say a word. He stared at Joel with a dark intensity. A flash distracted Joel. The twins continued laughing, staring out the living room window. Jason would not stop staring at his cousin. Another flash. Joel looked out the window himself. His jaw was agape as he saw a group of people taking pictures with their phones and camera's just like he and Jason had done very recently. The loud, piercing scream that he had heard in his condo was back. It sounded like it was coming closer, and much louder. He only had a second to think, as he looked up to see the woman with the long, flowing black hair, and the white gown, hovering over the four of them. Her left hand grabbed the back of Joel's head. Her right hand grabbed the back of Jason's head, ripping out a chunk of his hair. Another flash went off as Joel's head was snapped back, breaking his neck. The force was so strong, that the tendons in his neck ripped open, causing Joel to look like a PEZ Dispenser. The woman's scream became louder, and much angrier. The dark mist that was Lillian Lincoln became much bigger, enveloping both boys, causing the window to shatter.

14

"HOLY SHIT!"

"WHAT THE FUCK?"

"HOLY CHRIST!" were just some of the many reactions from the group of people taking pictures of the Lincoln House, as the window pane came crashing to the ground, and shards of glass went flying in many directions. Most of the group backed up in fear, as some continued taking pictures. A large, obese man wearing a 'GATEWAY TO HELL GHOST TOURS' t-shirt jumped off the bus and said,"Alright everyone. That's enough. Time to get back on the bus, and get the hell out of here. Not only do we have to worry about some angry spirits, but the local law enforcement can be just as scary! That was the FIRST and LAST time I ever let anyone off the bus at the Lincoln house! It's a goddamn lawsuit waiting to happen."

"Oh, come on Dan. Lighten up. It's finally starting to become interesting," said a young man taking pictures.

A few agreed with him. Another said,"Yeah, I want my money's worth."

Most of the group ran back to the bus, not wanting to know or see anything. Dan, the tour guide for 'Gateway to Hell Tours' walked up and down the aisle, taking a headcount. Some people were scared, others thought it was a stunt put for the tour, and still others were excited and wired.

"Alright, everyone is accounted for."
Speaking to the driver, "Dan said, "Now let's get the hell out of here!"
As the bus began slowly making its way down Paranormal Parkway, some yelled out, "Have you ever seen anything like........."
Cutting him off in mid-sentence, Dan blurted out, "NEVER! I have been doing this same tour for Christ knows how long, and I have never, I repeat NEVER, have seen anything remotely resembling what happened out there tonight."
Another passenger shot back,"Aw, come on Dan. We all know this was part of the tour. Nice touch, I might add."
"Excuse me sir," said Dan. What's your name?"
"Rob."
"Okay, Rob. I will swear on my mother's grave that I, or anyone affiliated with this tour had nothing to do with this. I've see alot of weird shit. Sorry, ma'am," he said to the older woman sitting in the front seat.
"As I was saying, I have seen and heard alot of STRANGE things on this tour, but NOTHING like this!"
The passengers began murmuring to themselves; some nervously laughing, others looking at their pictures, and a younger girl crying in the back. Two twenty something boys were going through the photos they took on their phone.
"Hey, Joe. You gotta see this," said one of the boys.

Joe grabbed his friend's I-Phone, and began to examine the picture in question. It was of the large window looking into the living room of the Lincoln House.

"Hey, is that the one that was covered with flies?" asked Joe.

"Yes, that would be the one."

"I don't see anything," said Joe.

"What? Are you fucking blind?!"

Joe's friend grabbed the phone, enlarged the photo, and handed it back.

"Look, right there," he said, pointing to a swirling black mist. A woman with long black hair, wearing a white gown could be seen coming out of the mist, hovering over two older boys, and two younger boys.

Joe looked closely. He took the phone away from his face, and exclaimed, "HOLY SHIT! Do we have ourselves a Family Portrait of the infamous Lincoln clan? Only one problem. I thought they only had two young boys, Billy and David. Who are the other two?"

"First of all, I, not we, have a family portrait of what must be the lovely Lincoln's. The other two could be cousins or friends. Who gives a shit who the fuck they are? On this camera is actual proof of the paranormal."

Joe stood up from his seat, and said, "Hey, Dan. Come here for a second. You're gonna want to see this."

Dan was busy speaking with the older couple up front as the bus bumped up and down, driving along the dirt road, departing Paranormal Parkway.

Joe spoke up louder. "Hey, Dan the Man. Can you come here. I have something to show you."

Dan looked up. "Yeah, I'll be there in a minute."

Joe became more insistent. "No, come now. I promise it will be worth your while."

Dan let out an exasperated breath.

"Ok, I'm on my way. Placing his hand on the shoulder of the woman he was speaking with, Dan said, "Sorry about the interruption. I'll be right back. As Dan began walking to the back, the bus bounced again on the rough terrain, causing him to lose his balance. He grabbed hold of the seat where the two boys were sitting, regaining control.

"Okay, boys. What's so damn important that it can't wait until later. If this bus hits anymore rough patches, I might end up being your tour guide as a specter."

A few passengers chuckled. Joe grabbed the phone out of his friend's hand. "Look at this!"

Dan held the phone in his left hand, as he used his right hand to steady himself by holding onto the seat. Seeing what the two boys were referring to almost immediately, he blurted out as if he was the only one on the bus, "THIS IS FUCKING GREAT!"

Dan swiped to the left. The mist became larger. He swiped again. This time he saw the woman coming out of the mist. Swiping a third time, he could see her head becoming larger, as her mouth was open in full scream mode. The next picture featured the woman grabbing the two older boys by the head. Similar to watching a cartoon by flipping through pages, his swiping was telling a story. The fifth picture consisted of the two heads nearly being decapitated by force.

Curious passengers were now leaving their seat, crowding around Dan, hoping to catch a glimpse of the photos.

"Alright, everyone has to sit down. I can't afford any lawsuits. I promise to post these unbelievable photos on my website later tonight."

After a few grunts and groans, everyone went back to their seats. Dan swiped to the right to look at a previous picture.

"This is clearly a picture of the Lincoln family, minus dear ol' dad. I know that the two younger boys are Billy and David, but why do the older boys look so damn familiar? I am horrible with names, but I never forget a face."

Dan made the picture bigger by zooming in on the two older boys.

"Damn it! I know these faces."

"Do you think it might be cousin's, or friends of the Lincoln's?" asked Joe.

Dan put the phone closer to his face, enlarging the picture even more.

"Dan."

No response. Joe said it much louder. "DAN!"

That snapped him out of it.

"Um, no. There were no relatives or friends that I am aware of, but goddamn it, I know those faces from somewhere."

15

35 miles away, an ambulance pulled into the parking lot of a condo complex. A slim woman, with a fair complexion, and shoulder length red hair, came running out of her condo towards the ambulance. "Right here! Right here!" she repeated, waving her arms. The ambulance stopped. A police cruiser pulled in right behind the ambulance. Both the officer and the paramedic got out.

"What's the problem ma'am?" asked the officer. "You seemed pretty frantic on the phone."

Slightly shaking, the woman responded, "I'm not exactly sure. but I heard very loud noises, and what sounded like a woman's scream, coming from the condo next to me."

"What kind of noises?" asked the officer, writing notes in a small pad that he took out from his back pocket.

"Again, I'm not sure, but there was a loud crash. I know my walls are super thin, but this crash was loud enough to rattle my walls."

The officer followed up with, "You wouldn't happen to know who lives there?"

As a matter fact, I do. A nice young gentleman. His name is Joel. Joel Gianni."

She seemed distracted as the officer continued writing in his notepad. She became fixated on the upstairs window of Joel Gianni's condo.

"Excuse me, ma'am, but I could really use your help."
She looked at the officer, seeming confused for a
second.

The officer continued. "How long have you known
him?"

"I've been living here since 2010. Great kid. Never
partied, that I know of. If he did, he kept it quiet. I
know that he worked alot."

"Where does he work?"

"Staples. Yes, he's the manager at Staples, right down
the road."

Thank you. I'll check with them to see if he worked
tonight. Did you see him tonight?"

"No. I had today off from work. It was such a crazy
week, that I didn't leave my condo all day. Caught up
on some well-needed rest."

"Thank you very much, ma'am."
The woman began to relax a bit.

"No need to call me ma'am. The name is Jane. Jane
Cavanaugh."

"Yarbro. Officer Paul Yarbro."

Jane extended her hand to Officer Yarbro. "And your
name is? she asked the paramedic.

"John McCauffrey, ma'am. Sorry. I mean Jane."

"Okay. Now that we have all of the pleasantries out
of the way, tell me what happened," sighed Officer
Yarbro.

"Where should I start?"

"The beginning. Let's start at the beginning."

16

As if on cue, a loud bang was heard in the upstairs window of Joel Gianni's condo. The three looked up at the same time.

"Okay, Jane. You stay here. John and I will be right back."

John opened the back of the ambulance, taking out the stretcher.

Wide-eyed, Jane asked, "What in God's name do you need that for?"

"Not that it's any concern of yours, but we like to be ready in cases where somebody is hurt," said Officer Yarbros.

"Yeah, but we don't know if he's hurt or not," said Jane.

Audibly sighing, Officer Yarbros said, "Fine. We like to be ready in case he might be hurt. It's called being proactive."

Yarbros and McCauffrey wheeled the stretcher to the small concrete stairwell leading to the front door. Jane was right behind them.

"I thought I told you to stay behind, "said Officer Yarbros, unconsciously touching his gun. "This is official police business. I'd hate to have John make some extra room for you in the ambulance."

Jane, not knowing if this was a threat or a promise, raised her two arms as if surrendering, backing down the three stairs to the parking lot.

"Alright, alright. I'll be right here if you need me."

"Greatly appreciated, ma'am, I mean Jane."
Officer Yarbros began knocking on the screen door.
"Joel, open up. This is Officer Yarbros. Are you alright? We are not here to harass you. Your lovely neighbor was worried about you. So are we."
No answer. John rang the doorbell. Jane was in the parking lot by the ambulance, looking up at the upstairs window.
"Do you hear anything?' she asked.
Officer Yarbros shook his head, not answering the question.
"Excuse me, he said, pushing John out of the way. "I want to open the screen door."
John moved to the side as Officer Yarbros opened the screen door, now pounding his heavy fist on the inside door made of oak.
"Open up. This is Officer Yarbros."
A succession of three rapid knocks yielded no response. His patience was at an all-time low.
"Joel Gianni. Once again, this is Officer Yarbros. If you don't open this damn door, I'll gladly do it for you!"
No response, but another loud bang was heard upstairs.
"That's it! Move aside one more time, John."
Paul grabbed the railing, lifting his right leg up, giving the door a swift kick. It didn't budge. Still holding onto the railing for leverage, Paul gave the door another kick.

It moved somewhat, but not enough to open the door. John moved back to the top step, and said, "Excuse me, Officer Yarbros. Let me have a try."
Officer Yarbros, aged 54, grossly overweight, and out of shape, was bent over, breathing heavily.
"Alright, John. Let's see what you got."
Paul backed down the three steps to the parking lot, giving John some room. John turned sideways, his left side facing the door. Instead of using his leg to kick the door, he rammed his left shoulder into the door. A piece of the wood cracked. He stepped back, charging at the door, thrusting his left shoulder into the door. More wood was cracked.
From the bottom of the stairs, Officer Yarbros said, "Come on, John. One more time, and we're in!"
John stepped back, and charged forward again, ramming into the door. Officer Yarbros was correct. The door opened all the way, hanging only by a hinge. John and Paul both walked inside. Empty beer bottles littered the kitchen table, along with a Ouija Board and planchette. John picked up the planchette out of curiosity, as Paul began examining the hole in the wall.
"What the fuck happened here?" asked Officer Yarbros.
Looks like a possible home invasion to me," answered John.
Looking into the living room, the two noticed CD's and DVD's strewn about the place.
"This place is a fucking mess!" said John.

"Holy shit! I'm afraid you are correct, John. This definitely looks like a home invasion."

Another loud bang came from upstairs. No words needed to be spoken as the two ran up the stairs. They both turned the corner at the top to the left. The bathroom light was on. Inside the tub, lay 25-year-old Joel Gianni, his face covered in blood, pieces of his front teeth lying in the tub.

"What monster would do this?" asked John in disgust.

He had seen his share of carnage in the 15 years he was a paramedic, but nothing this grotesque in a very long time. Joel's right side of his skull was bashed in from hitting the side of the tub. His torso was twisted like a pretzel.

"Let's get this damn thing out of here!" said Officer Yarbros, pointing at the body. I'm going to call for back-up. I have a feeling that I'll be here all night."

John ran down the stairs to grab his stretcher. He opened the screen door, hitting Jane in the face. He ran past her, not offering an apology or explanation. Officer Paul Yarbros walked slowly and steadily down the stairs. He opened the screen door, placing his hand on Jane's shoulder, pushing her to the side.

"What did I tell you about staying out of the way? This is Official Police Business. You wouldn't want to be arrested for obstruction of justice, would you?"

Jane placed her left hand on her nose, where she had been hit by the screen door, saying nothing. Officer Yarbros repeated himself, "Now do you?"

"N-N-N-No officer," she stammered.

"Great. Now will you kindly get the fuck out of the way?!"

Jane walked down to the parking lot, as John brought the stretcher to the stairs.

"Hey, can you grab the other side?" he asked Officer Yarbros.

They carried the stretcher inside, rested a second before carrying it up the 13 stairs leading to the bathroom.

"Alright. Leave it here," said John referring to the small hallway leading from the bathroom to the bedroom.

"Officer Yarbros stepped inside the bathroom, pinching his nose.

"Jesus Christ. This stinks!"

John walked past him, to the body in the tub. "Here, put these on," he said, handing Officer Yarbros a pair of vinyl gloves, and a mask to cover his face.

Putting them on, he gingerly bent over to grab the twisted and bloodied body. John grabbed the legs, as Paul grabbed underneath the two armpits.

"Okay. Slowly, slowly," said John placing the body on the stretcher.

17

No words were spoken as the two men carried the stretcher down the stairs, stopping at the door. Waiting at the screen door was Jane. She opened the screen door, making it easier for the two men to carry the stretcher outside. She gasped, putting her hand over her mouth, as the body was moved down the stairs to the ambulance.

Running over to the ambulance, Jane stuttered,"Wh-wh-wh- what happened? Was he murdered?"

Officer Yarbros removed his vinyl gloves and face mask. "I thought I told you to stay the fuck out of the way!"

Visibly shaken, Jane said, "I-I-I- have a right to know if there is a killer loose in this complex. We all do, "she continued, sweeping her arm in a giant arc, indicating that she meant the entire complex.

"Listen. As soon as I find out what the fuck is going on, I will be sure to contact you. Right now, we don't have a fucking clue. We know about as much as you do."

As Officer Yarbros made his proclamation, John McCauffrey opened the back of the ambulance, stepped up, and began pulling the stretcher into the ambulance. Officer Yarbros watched him struggle for a few seconds before grabbing the other side of the stretcher, and helped lift it onto the ambulance.

"Thank you sir," said John.

"Don't mention it."

Looking around and not seeing Jane, John said, "Hey, it looks like your new friend found a hobby, and decided to finally leave you alone."

It's about fucking time. She's more annoying than my wife!"

A loud, hideous scream was heard from inside the condo, followed by a smaller, but no less hideous scream, followed by a loud bang.

"Shit! Looks like Gladys Kravitz found something where she has no business being."

"Why do you assume it's her?" asked John.

"My 20 years on the force tells me that I am correct."

"Do you want me to stick around?"

Officer Yarbros looked at his watch, and said, "Nah, there's no use of the two of us being stuck here all night. You have what you need. Now let me go get what I need."

"Are you sure?"

Yeah. Besides, back-up should be here soon."

"Alright. You don't have to tell me twice, said John, closing the back of the ambulance, jumping into the driver's seat, and starting it up. Officer Yarbros began walking back to the condo, swearing under his breath. John beeped twice, waving as he drove out of the parking lot into the street.

Officer Yarbros gave a quick wave and continued walking up the steps to the door.

Opening the door, he almost vomited at what he saw. Inside, at the bottom of the stairs, lay Jane Cavanaugh's body.

The torso was completely twisted; the two legs bent backward at the knee, with bones piercing through the skin. The body was lying face down, with her head twisted a complete 180. Jane's face was looking up at Officer Yarbros with a mummified scream. The two arms were broken in at least 13 different places.

"What the fu.."

Officer Yarbros was interrupted by a loud bang coming from the bathroom. He grabbed the walkie talkie attached to his belt. Pressing down on the button, he spoke into the talkie.

"This is Officer Yarbros. Please send back-up. Possible 187. Looking at the body, he clicked the button again.

"Make that a definite 187 of two victims."

The dispatcher responded, "Will do. Officer Yarbros. Several cars are on their way now."

"Thanks Bea."

As he returned the walkie talkie to his belt, he heard another loud bang from upstairs. He grabbed the gun from its holster, now holding it in his right hand. Looking at the gun, then upstairs, he said as if speaking to the gun, "Let's go!"

18

He ran up the stairs as fast as a 285-pound man could, making a left into the bathroom. Nothing seemed out of the ordinary. Everything was as he left it, minus one slight difference: the shower curtain was closed.

"That's odd. I don't remember closing it, "he said to himself.

Walking over to the tub, he slipped on some blood that was on the floor. Grabbing the towel rack was the only thing that prevented his fat ass from hitting the floor.

"Shit!" he said, breathing heavily.

It took a few seconds to regain his composure. Standing in front of the tub, he grabbed hold of the curtain, and pulled it open. All of his insides turned into liquid shit as he saw a younger woman with long black hair, wearing a white gown, staring back at him with a sinister grin. Her teeth were rotting, and a pungent smell emanated from her mouth. Like David Copperfield performing a magic trick, he quickly closed the curtain, as if doing this would make the woman disappear. He looked down at the gun in his right hand. Smiling now, and feeling more confident, he held the gun straight ahead, tearing open the shower curtain once again.

"FREEZE BITCH!"

The woman was now transparent. Opening her mouth, she let out a loud, hideous scream. Officer Yarbros shot three times without even thinking. The bullets went right through the transparent woman, hitting the wall. Her mouth opened wider, as if her jaw was enlarging. The scream became louder as she jumped out at Officer Yarbros. He didn't have time to scream as his head was ripped completely clear from his body.

19

A small crowd was now gathering outside as two police cruisers pulled into the parking lot. The two officers parked, and stepped out of their cars. "Alright, everyone. Show's over. Everyone back inside," one officer said, as they ascended the stairs into the condo of Joel Gianni.

THE END

TAKIN' CARE OF BUSINESS

34-year-old Tommy Wozniak knew it was going to be a great day. Why wouldn't it be? He just began a 2-week vacation from a job that he loved, had a gorgeous girlfriend, and most importantly, he was spending his first day of vacation at The Chiller Convention in New Jersey. The Chiller Convention is named after Chiller Theater, which aired horror movies back in the 1970's. The Convention originally only featured horror stars from the past, but more recently morphed into a pop culture extravaganza, featuring all of his favorite television and movie stars from the 1960's, 1970's and the 1980's. Past guests that Tommy felt lucky enough to meet included stars from 'Happy Days', 'Laverne and Shirley', 'WKRP in Cincinnati', 'What's Happening', and many more from his favorite era. Many of his friends accused him of being nostalgic, but he would proudly pit any of those shows up against the shit (as he called it) they air now. Tommy was also a huge horror fan, which began at a very early age. He was only 10 when his father took him to see his All-Time favorite horror film, 'Phantasm'. By age 12 he had seen every horror film from 'JAWS' to 'The Exorcist'. Instead of being afraid, the exact opposite happened. He became jaded, and fascinated with everything horror. Tommy's love didn't end with American horror. He also enjoyed the Italian Classics from Lucio Fulci, and Dario Argento.

His love for cinema greatly intensified after he began going to these horror movie convention's; getting to meet and speak with the people that helped create some of his favorite movies.

2

Tommy knew that he had met his soulmate when he was introduced to Jessica Peterson at a party. Not only was she beautiful, but she was wearing an 'Exorcist' shirt. They immediately clicked. Tommy and Jessica became inseparable. She was 33 years old, but loved all of the same television shows and movies that Tommy did. Many of their friends thought the two were crazy when they mentioned that they wished they were older. Their friends would surmise, 'Why would you want to wish your life away like that? 'Tommy and Jessica would laugh off their clueless friends. They didn't want to wish their life away at all, they just wanted to live in a time when life seemed much better, more fun, and music, movies and television were at their finest.

3

Tommy looked at the clock on his nightstand in his condo. The time read: 7:15am. He told Jessica that he would pick her up at 8:00am. The Convention opened its doors at 11am. It was a two-hour drive, and he didn't want to miss a second of Chiller. He jumped in the shower, got dressed, wearing his 'Phantasm' shirt, of course, and made his way to Jessica's.

Tommy drove up to the curb in front of Jessica's parent's house. She recently moved back in with her parents and her younger brother Eric. After she graduated college, she moved in with several friends into a very small apartment. She loved the independence of being on her own, but hated the fact that she didn't have any privacy, and all of her money was going into a place that she would never own. Jessica luckily had a great relationship with her parents. They told her she could live at home rent-free until she had saved enough money to buy a condo of her own.

Tommy beeped the car horn. Nothing.

"Come on," Tommy said impatiently. He looked at the clock on his car dashboard. The time read: 7:57am.

"I don't want to be late," he said as he laid his hand on the horn once again. No movement in the house that he could see.

"Ugggghhhh," he sighed, as he got out of his car and walked up to the front door. At first, he tried the doorbell. This had the same response as the horn did. His patience already worn thin, Tommy opened up the screen door and began knocking furiously on the white oak door.

"Be right there," came a female voice from inside. The voice calmed him down. It was Jessica. There stood Jessica; tall, thin, flowing black hair that went to the lower portion of her back, wearing an 'Evil Dead' shirt. Tommy took one look at the shirt, and blurted out, "GROOVY," which is a catchphrase of the protagonist 'Ash' in the movie.

"Give Me Some Sugar Baby," said Jessica, as she pulled Tommy forward, kissing him on the lips.

"DISGUSTING!" came a voice from behind Jessica. It was her 15-year-old brother, Eric. He was overly tall for his age, gangly, and extremely skinny. His pants were too short for his long legs, causing his white socks to ride up his legs. He had thick glasses with a black frame.

"There is nothing disturbing about this at all, you Urkel wannabe!" said Tommy, planting another kiss on Jessica's lips.

Even though Eric was only 15, he understood that Urkel was a reference to the unfunny comedy 'Family Matters', that reigned supreme back in the 90's. Jessica gave Tommy a small love tap on the shoulder.

"Come on, Tommy. Leave him alone. That mad genius will be running the world someday, and I would highly recommend that you stay on his good side."

"Yeah," said Tommy. "What are you doing downstairs all day, you demented Simon Bar Sinister?"

"He may have gotten the Urkel reference, but I am guessing that 'UnderDog' is far too in the past for Eric to pick up that reference," laughed Jessica. "Come on. Let's get out of here."

"That's the best idea that I have heard all day," said Tommy. "Have fun becoming Master of the Universe, Alfalfa."

Eric didn't understand that reference as well, but he knew that it was derogatory. Eric understood that ANYTHING and EVERYTHING out of Tommy's mouth was sarcastic.

Eric didn't say a word. He stood behind his sister, staring with extreme hatred for Jessica's boyfriend. He couldn't understand what she could possibly see in that uneducated Cro-Magnon.

Tommy could feel Eric's stare.

"Calm down, Einstein. You know that I am just kidding. What's the matter? Can't take a joke? If you can't do that, you will never survive in this world; Evil Genius, or No Evil Genius!"

Without waiting for a reply, Tommy and Jessica walked out the house, closing the front door.

Once in the car, and on their way to the Convention. Tommy said, "Are you 100% positive that the Demon Seed known as your brother, came from the same spawn?"

"Give him a chance. He will grow on you," laughed Jessica.

"Yeah, like a fungus! What the hell does he actually do downstairs all day?"

He's extremely secretive," said Jessica. "One time, I went downstairs to let him know that dinner was ready. I caught a quick glimpse of eight or nine experiments that he had set up. I was unable to see what they were, before he began freaking out, screaming for me to go upstairs. He literally chased me upstairs. I'm twice his age, but the little bugger scares the crap out of me!"

"What do your parents say?"

"Well, since he is so much younger, and he was an accident, mom and dad tend to spoil him rotten. He's become like Billy Mumy's character in that classic 'Twilight Zone' episode. You know the one where you can't have any bad thoughts, or you will be banished to the cornfield."

"I know it well," said Tommy with a sense of pride. 'The Twilight Zone' is my favorite show, and that's my favorite episode."

"Aw, forget about him," said Jessica. "Let's go have some fun."

"Malachai is forgotten!"

"How do you manage to turn every situation into a horror movie reference?" asked Jessica, referring to his 'Children of the Corn' reference.

"It's a talent, baby," he shot back sarcastically.

4

Tommy and Jessica arrived at Chiller just as the long line outside was beginning to move. Once parked, and inside, they met many celebrities from their favorite shows. This year included the cast of 'Three's Company', 'Leave it To Beaver' and 'The Dukes of Hazard'. Some of the stars from the Silver Screen included: Danny Glover, Linda Hamilton, and Martin Landau. Sadly, weeks later, it would prove to be one of Landau's final public appearances, as he died from natural causes.

Tommy and Jessica were having such a great time hobnobbing with all of the celebrities; taking pictures, and going back and forth quoting lines from their favorite movies. Jessica took out her phone to check the time.

"OK, what's next? We met everyone we wanted to meet, and even some that I wish we didn't. You have to admit that Linda Hamilton is a real bitch!"

I can't, and I won't, deny that," said Tommy. "Anyway, what's next is my favorite part of the day: the Vendor Room. Let's go purchase some horror merchandise."

"More?" asked Jessica incredulously. "Your condo already looks more like a museum than a place to live. I am always expecting your little figures to come to life, and kill you in your sleep!"

Tommy laughed at this. "Oh, they will kill," he joked. "But only for me. They are my Horror Secret Service."

"Keep telling yourself that!" said Jessica. I don't want to be the person that finds your dead body."

Tommy laughed again. "Yeah, you would call the police and paramedics ONLY after you emptied my condo of all my DVD's into your trunk."

Jessica gave him a love tap on the shoulder. "Only my favorites. Make sure you make 'Phantasm' and 'The Evil Dead Trilogy' easy to find."

They both laughed at this as they walked down the long corridor leading to the vendor room.

They walked from vendor to vendor, admiring the vast array of DVD's, posters, movie soundtracks, and t-shirts. Miraculously, they made it to the final table without purchasing a single item.

"Wow! This is a first!" exclaimed Jessica. "We might actually go home without buying a single piece of merchandise."

It was at that exact moment that Tommy saw the miniature coffin on the vendors table. It was all black, approximately 2 feet long. The vendor gave Tommy a huge smile as he and Jessica walked up to the table.

"You like this?" he said to Tommy.

"Hell yeah! This would make a perfect addition to my collection."

Tommy noticed a cord on the side of the coffin.

"What does this do?" he said, pointing at the cord.

The vendor's smile widened as he grabbed the cord.

"This is what makes it the perfect addition to ANY collection."

Tommy stared at it, as if in a trance, waiting in anticipation. The vendor knew he had him right where he wanted him. He began toying with Tommy. "Do you wanna see what it does?"

"Hell yeah!" seemed to be the only 2 words that once again Tommy could put together to form a cohesive sentence.

The vendor plugged it into a power cord underneath his table. A small whirring noise began, followed by a miniature bony hand from inside the coffin raising the lid. This was followed by a high, nasally voice crying out 'HELP ME!' The hand then closed the lid. Tommy watched in awe as the skeleton inside raised the lid, cried out 'HELP ME', and closed it again several times. He could watch it all day. After the 5th time, he blurted out, "I'll take it!"

Jessica put her arm around Tommy. "Honey, don't be so impulsive. You don't even know how much it costs."

"I don't care how much it costs. That's what this is for," said Tommy, taking out his credit card. "A small coffin, with a miniature body pleading 'HELP ME' in Vincent Price's voice from 'The Fly'. I MUST HAVE THIS!!!!"

Jessica knew it was useless to argue with him. Once he made up his mind, that was it, and besides, it was kind of cool, she thought to herself.

"Only $100.00," said the vendor. "But, you know what? I love someone that can appreciate the classics. I'll sell it to you for the low price of $75.00." He wasn't even done speaking as Tommy dropped the credit card on the table, and blurted out, "Deal!"

5

The ride home was spent with the two of them reminiscing about their favorite, and least favorite celebrities. Linda Hamilton came up again. Mostly, Tommy went on and on about how cool his new toy was.

"You'll have to show Eric. He will love it," said Jessica.

"Why would I show that future madman anything?"

"Because, if you are nice enough to show him your cool, new toy, then I will be nice enough to show you these toys," said Jessica pulling her shirt down, exposing her breasts.

"Yeah, you're right. Eric is gonna love this!" said Tommy as he pressed his foot on the gas pedal.

6

Tommy and Jessica pulled up to Jessica's parents' house at approximately 9pm. All of the lights were out, including the porch light.

"That's odd," said Jessica. "It doesn't look like anyone is home."

"No complaints there," said Tommy, putting his arm around Jessica, pulling her closer, and kissing her on the cheek. "Hotel Peterson is Open for Business," he added, grabbing her breast.

"You're like the love child of Hugh Hefner and an octopus," she said, pushing him off of her.

"I'll take that as a compliment."

"For some strange reason, I knew you would. Come on. Let's see if anyone is home, then MAYBE, I'm saying a huge MAYBE, we can play National Geographic."

"I love it when you talk dirty," laughed Tommy.

Jessica was already at the house door, searching for her keys as Tommy was getting out of his car.

"Hey. Don't forget to bring your new toy inside to show Eric," yelled Jessica.

Tommy gave a disgruntled look, until Jessica pulled her 'Evil Dead' shirt down again, exposing the top of her cleavage. The disgruntled look quickly turned into a smile as he grabbed the coffin, and walked inside the house with Jessica.

"Mom. Dad. Eric. Is anyone home?" asked Jessica. She walked down the hallway, calling them again. No answer.

"See, no one is here. Let's make Casa Peterson mucho caliente!" laughed Tommy, as he wrapped both arms around Jessica, kissing her on the neck. She closed her eyes, relaxing, and enjoying the moment. Loud music, blaring from downstairs, was an instant mood killer. She opened her eyes, pushing Tommy off of her.

"Hey.....," he started to say, but stopped as the cellar door opened, and Eric walked out.

"Well," if it isn't Romeo and Juliet?" asked Eric, disgustedly.

"That would be 'Tromeo and Juliet', you maniacal minion," shot back Tommy.

"What the heck is 'Tromeo and Juliet'?"

"Only one of the best low-budget movies of All-Time, but of course you wouldn't know that. The only thing that interests you is whatever you haven't hidden in your Secret Lair," mocked Tommy.

Jessica, attempting to avoid the two of them from fighting, jumped into the conversation by grabbing the coffin and saying,"Hey, Eric. Look at this cool toy Tommy bought."

"Yeah, yeah, yeah," said Eric, dismissing it with a wave of his left hand.

Jessica continued. "No, I'm serious. Look at this."

184

She plugged the coffin in. The whirring began. The bony hand opened the coffin very slowly, whining in that high- pitched Vincent Price fly voice, 'HELP ME'. The hand slowly lowered the lid. Eric stood watching it, hoping Tommy and his sister didn't notice how cool he actually thought it was.

"Too bad it wasn't bigger. We could put Tommy in there," said Eric.

"Yeah, very funny Padre. That will never happen!" said a visibly annoyed Tommy.

"I've seen stranger things happen," said Eric. "Wait. I take that back. You are, by far, the strangest thing I have ever seen. If I ever took you to school, I would definitely get an A+ on my Science Project. The subject would be,'What is the Missing Link'?

"ALRIGHT!" shouted Jessica louder than they expected, even louder than she expected.

They both immediately shut up. Seizing the moment to change the conversation, Jessica added, "Where's Mom and Dad? I don't see the car."

"I'm not sure. They mentioned something about getting something to eat, and going somewhere after. I'm not sure. I wasn't listening. It pisses me off. They knew I had plans."

"Aw, poor baby," said Tommy.

Jessica didn't have to say a word. She shot him a dirty look. He knew enough to stop.

"Speaking of getting something to eat, what's for dinner, sis?"

Jessica looked at her brother. "I'm not sure. Let's see what's in the fridge. Tommy, are you hungry? You are more than welcome to stay."

Tommy realizing that his Night of Passion was ruined, shrugged his shoulders and said, "No, that's ok. I'm all set."

Jessica, now looking disappointed, gave him a hug and a kiss on the cheek, and said, "Alright. Give me a call when you get home. I want to make sure you get home safely."

"Yes, honey. Please do that!" mocked Eric.

Tommy's face became bright red with anger. He opened his mouth to say something to Eric, when Jessica said, "Talk to you soon, honey," pushing Tommy toward the front door.

Once outside, Tommy blurted out, "Your brother is a real asshole, you know that???!!!"

"What I do know is that you are a kind, forgiving, mature adult that doesn't let a 15 year old Evil Genius rattle him."

A smile appeared on Tommy's face as he recited a line from another of his favorite movies 'The Warriors',"ONE TOUGH CHICK!"

Jessica laughed, and followed up with another line from the same movie,"Can You Dig It?"

"Oh, you know I can definitely do that," he said, as his hand grazed her ass.

"Great. I'll see you tomorrow. Text me when you get home."

7

Jessica opened the door, holding it open until Tommy started the car, and pulled away. She waved, watching him drive down the road. Once inside, she saw that Eric had returned to doing whatever the hell it was he did downstairs. She found some leftovers from the family's night at Senor Pancho's, and began to heat it up.

"Mexican Night it is!"

Once the burrito's, nacho's and beans were sufficiently cooked, she opened up the cellar door, yelling for Eric to come upstairs. Jessica's voice was drowned out by the stereo downstairs blaring The Zombies classic, 'Time of the Season'.

"That's fitting," muttered Jessica to herself.

She began walking downstairs. Her left foot reached the 4th step when Eric came running around the corner yelling,"What the hell are you doing down here? This is private!"

Jessica took one more step, prompting Eric to run up the stairs, stopping his older sister from going any further.

Eric exclaimed," I'm serious. You don't see me going through your private stuff."

"Alright. Alright. I just wanted to let you know that down there it might be 'Time of the Season', but up here it's 'Time of the Burrito'. Why do you always have that stereo blasting so loud anyway?"

"Playing Classic Rock helps me think."

"I'm not sure how anyone can think with music, Classic or not, that loud."
"Whatever," was Eric's response. "Let's go upstairs." Eric followed Jessica upstairs as The Zombies morphed into Warren Zevon's 'Werewolves of London'.

8

It wasn't until Tommy arrived at his condo that he had realized that he had forgotten his brand new toy. He punched his steering wheel with his fist. "Shit! I can't believe that I forgot to bring it with me. That motherfucker Eric better keep his dirty paws off of it."

He grabbed his phone out of his back pocket to dial Jessica's cell. The time read 10:15pm.

"She better answer the phone."

Tommy knew all too well that Jessica liked to be in bed early. Not only did she like it, but she was unable to stay awake past 10pm. It didn't matter where she was, or what she was doing. He once bought tickets for the two of them to see a live stage version of The Who's Rock Opera, 'Tommy'. He noticed her nodding off during the performance. Halfway through 'Pinball Wizard' she was in full sleep mode. When the song was finished, it received a loud applause. She woke up out of a dead sleep, stood up, and gave it a standing ovation. She thought that the Rock Opera had ended. Another time, she fell asleep in mid-conversation at Caroline's Comedy Club. He knew that the chances of her still being awake were slim to none. He dialed the phone. It rang once."Come on, Jessica. I don't want my coffin left with your psycho brother!"

2 rings. Nothing. 3 rings. Nothing.

After the 4th, the voicemail kicked in. 'Hi. This is Jessica. Leave your name and number after the beep.'

"Hey babe, it's me. Please pick up. It's important." Tommy hung up the phone after leaving the message, and immediately called back. After the 4th ring, he left another message. "Come on Jessica. Answer the damn phone. I want my coffin back." He hung up, and dialed again. After the 4th ring he left another message.

"I don't care if you are asleep or not, I'm on my way to pick up my new toy!"

Tommy laughed to himself at how ridiculous he sounded. He began mocking himself. Speaking in a small, child-like voice he said, "Hey, Jessica, my mommy really hates when the other kids play with my toys. I need to pick them up immediately." Cracking himself up, Tommy continued in the child's voice, using a different scenario:

"Hey, Jessica. After I'm done playing with my G.I. Joe dolls, I'll be over to pick up my toy."

Even as he admitted to himself how ludicrous it sounded, he still felt a sense of urgency bringing the coffin back to the condo. Currently parked in the condo parking lot, he started the car, turned on the radio, and began his drive back to Jessica's. The traffic was light. He was there in record time. All of the houselights were still off. Tommy began looking for Jessica's parent's car. The only car in the driveway was Jessica's silver Chevy Celebrity.

"What the hell? They can't still be out!"
Tommy parked his car in the driveway behind Jessica's, and walked to the door. He opened up the screen door, and began pounding on the wooden door.
"Hey, let me in. Jessica are you still up?"
The house was quiet. He began pounding even harder.
"Jessica, wake up. I know what a light sleeper you are."
Still nothing. He turned the doorknob to the left. To his surprise, the door opened. Tommy looked around for any sign of life, as he entered the house.
"Hello, Jessica. Mr. and Mrs. Peterson. Is anyone here?"
Tommy walked through the living room, the kitchen, and down the hall to the bathroom. No one seemed to be home.
"This is bat shit crazy!"
He walked 3 steps on the stairwell to Jessica's bedroom, when he noticed that the light to the basement was on. He stopped. Even though he knew the smarter thing to do was to wake up Jessica first, he felt a compulsion to see what Eric was doing.
"Yeah, let's see what the little freak is up to," Tommy laughed to himself.
He knew Eric would have a conniption if he saw him walking downstairs, so he opened the door slowly, and began walking silently.

Santana's 'Evil Woman' was blaring through the speakers. Tommy relaxed. There was no way in hell that Eric, or anyone, would hear him walking downstairs. Not that he was worried about pissing off Eric. He was more concerned with upsetting Jessica. She loathed confrontation, and hated it even more watching her loved one's fight or argue. It's not like he never tried getting along with Eric. He really did try. It just that it seemed like he was the only one that put any kind of effort into it. Every time that he attempted to be nice to the little snot, Eric would say something sarcastic. Tommy eventually gave up, and decided to fight sarcasm with sarcasm. He loved the battles of wit; not that he saw it as much of a battle, but when it upset Jessica, it upset him. Tommy was a real softie at heart.

9

Tommy walked further down the stairs, free from worry about the creaking noises they made. The music was at full blast as he reached the bottom step. He stopped, and stared in awe at what he saw. It all became clear why 'Dr. Evil' didn't want anyone downstairs. The cellar had numerous shelves filled with large, clear glass containers. They covered every square inch of space. One container had what looked like a guinea pig floating in formaldehyde. Another container housed a small ferret. A third container had a white rabbit floating in formaldehyde.

"Why you sick little fuck!"

Just as he made that comment, the song ended. Eric looked over to the staircase. It took several seconds for it to register that someone had violated his Secret Space.

"What the hell are you doing down here? Get the fuck out!" shouted Eric.

The words came out of Eric with such force and anger, that it surprised both Tommy and Eric.

"Forget that," said Tommy. I have a question for you, you devious, mentally ill Cro-Magnon. What the fuck are you doing with all of these dead animals floating around in your jars?"

Eric looked around at all of his 'experiment's, but remained silent.

"Answer me, you little prick!"

Tommy noticed 2 medium-sized boxes on a shelf. They were not clear.

"Alright," he continued. "If you can't, or won't answer that, tell me what the hell is in here."

Tommy picked up one box. It was light, but definitely had something in it. He shook it. Eric rushed at him. Tommy easily pushed him away. Eric ran back at him.

"Get the fuck away from me, kid!" he said, pushing Eric away one more time.

"Let's see what we have here," said Tommy, reaching his right hand inside the box.

He put his left hand over his mouth, his stomach convulsed, producing a dry-heave as he stared at the contents. In his right hand, he was holding Jessica's mother's severed head, by a clump of her auburn hair. She was staring back at him with her eyes and mouth wide open, as if screaming. The urge to empty the contents of his stomach all over the floor occurred once again, but something didn't seem right. There wasn't any blood, or any rancid smell, that is usually accompanied with a dead body. Not that Tommy had ever seen a dead body in person, but he read enough books, and had seen enough documentaries to know what it 'should' be like.

"What the fuck?" said Tommy, confused and disgusted, as he reached for the other box.

Eric yelled, "NO! Get away from there!"

"I'm not going anywhere. You're the one going away. Jail or asylum, not sure which one, but you will pay for this!"

As Tommy opened the 2nd box, he said, "Let me guess, you piece of shit. In here is what's left of your dad."

By now, Eric stood motionless, and defeated. There was no use in explaining to him what it was.

Tommy looked to his right as he dropped the head on the ground. On a shelf was his coffin with a yellow sticky note reading 'MISSING LINK' attached to it. He began to walk over to it.

"Why you John Wayne Gacy, Silence of the Lambs, thieving motherfucker!"

The instant that he grabbed the coffin, he felt a sharp pain in the back of his head, accompanied by a bright light. The coffin dropped to the floor. Tommy turned around to see Eric seething; his face bright red, breathing hard, holding a lead pipe in his right hand, ready to swing again.

"You're dead, you piece of shit!" screamed Tommy. He rushed at Eric. Eric swung the pipe like he was Babe Ruth swinging for the fences. The pipe connected with the right side of Tommy's skull. He faltered a bit, not quite falling down. He placed his hand on the large gash that was now oozing blood. Feeling dizzy, and confused, he once again rushed at Eric.

This time Eric swung the pipe up and down, like he was Paul Bunyan swinging his axe. The metal bar cracked open the top of Tommy's head. Blood immediately began gushing into his face and eyes. He attempted to wipe the blood away, but it was pouring out of the gash, much too quickly, like a water faucet. As fast as he could wipe the blood from his eyes, more entered. He could barely see. It was also creeping into his mouth. Tommy was wiping and spitting blood, waving his arms wildly, walking forward, looking for Eric like a demented Frankenstein.

"Where are you, you psycho?"

Tommy received his answer with a loud WHAAP to the head. This time, all he encountered was complete darkness, as his body hit the floor.

10

The sun shone brightly through Jessica's window. She blinked rapidly, groaning as the sun hit her face, waking her up. She rolled over in her bed, picking up her phone to check the time.

"8:25," she said to herself. "This is way too early to be up on a Saturday!"

Jessica threw her legs over the side of the bed, groaning as her sleepy joints began to crack as she stood up. It took several seconds for the grogginess to disappear, and all of yesterday's memories to come flooding back: the Convention, Eric and Tommy arguing, her parents.

'That's odd,' she thought to herself. 'Mom and dad always come upstairs to say goodnight, asleep or not.'

The sense of concern was only a flash as she said out loud, "They must have gone straight to bed once they got back home. Neither are night people, and I didn't get to sleep until sometime after 10."

Jessica stretched her arms to the ceiling, groaning, as her muscles began to awaken. Squinting out her bedroom window due to the bright sun, she looked in the driveway for her parent's car. The sense of concern returned when she didn't see their car, and even more disturbing was the fact that Tommy's car was in the driveway. Opening up her bedroom door, she began going through the house. There was no one to be found.

"What the fuck?"

The music of 'Sweet Home Alabama' was blasting from the downstairs speakers. Jessica ran down the staircase, to the basement.

"Is he fucking deaf? How loud does he need it?" she asked disgustedly to herself.

Opening the basement door, she screamed, "Eric, where's mom and dad. Why is Tommy's car here?"

No answer. Of course, there was no answer. Eric had the music so loud, Jessica wouldn't be surprised to see a live band playing.

"Eric. Turn that damn music down!"

Knowing that there wasn't a chance in Hell that Eric would be able to hear her, she began walking down the stairs. She made it to the 5th step, when a strong stench hit her like a Mack Truck.

"Oh my God, does that stink. Is this where he hides the bodies?" asked Jessica, nervously laughing.

She reached the bottom of the stairs, turning her head to the right. Eric had his hands-on Tommy's coffin, as if inspecting it. Opening it up, closing it, opening it up again. The smile on his face was eerie, almost sinister. Jessica walked over to him, undetected. The smile turned into surprise and shock, as she grabbed his shoulders, turning him around to face her.

She had so many questions. She began to ask him what he was doing with Tommy's coffin, when she noticed that Eric's clothes had what looked like blood, splattered all over his shirt and pants.

He stood there, unable to move or speak. Jessica had one hand on each of his shoulders, as she attempted to get some answers. The music was too loud. How was Eric going to hear her when she couldn't even hear herself think? She let him go to turn down the stereo. Just as she turned the music down to a manageable level, she stopped dead in her tracks. Jessica heard a small whirring noise as the coffin began to slowly open. Eric wanted to stop her from watching, but felt paralyzed. She watched as a small hand began to lift open the coffin from the inside. The hand looked much more realistic than what she saw yesterday. She suddenly remembered why. During yesterday's demonstration at the Convention, the hand was that of a skeleton. This hand was flesh and bones. She watched in horror as a shrunken version of Tommy slowly opened the coffin. The head had a large gash on the right side of his face, and the top of his skull. His mouth was wide open, reminiscent of Edvard Munch's 'Scream' The words 'HELP ME' were uttered. This time it wasn't Vincent Price from 'The Fly'. This was the voice of a terrified Tommy. The miniature Tommy slowly brought the lid down. He began to raise the lid again. "HELP M..." Tommy was cut off as Eric slammed the coffin shut. 'Sweet Home Alabama' came to an end as 'Bad Company's 'Feel Like Making Love' began playing. Jessica screamed, "What the fuck have you done?!" Eric walked over to the other side of the room.

Anything to get away from his angry, older sister. Tommy began lifting up the lid once again. "HELP ME."

Jessica snapped back to reality. She had read about the Jivaroan Tribes in the Amazon rainforest shrinking heads as trophies, but thought all of it was pure science fiction. She even bought Eric a book on the tribe last Christmas, thinking it was a funny joke. Now she stood watching what looked like her boyfriend closing the lid on a miniature coffin. She touched his face, as in disbelief. It was real, FUCKING REAL!

"You sick little voodoo child. What the hell, and how the fuck, did you do this?"

Eric had no answer. He stood by the two brown boxes, as if trying to hide them from her.

"What do you have in there?" she asked, still in shock, not entirely sure what was happening.

Eric stood in the corner with a smirk on his face, not saying a word. Jessica pushed him to the side. Looking down into the box, she was horrified to see her father's severed head staring back at her. Eric stumbled backwards, tripping over the other box. Their mother's severed head rolled across the floor, only stopping after hitting a wall.

Jessica snapped. "I'll fucking kill you!"

You don't understand. Tommy was going to kill me."

"What I do understand is that you are a cold-blooded murderer, killing 3 lives that I know of. How could you kill Mom and Dad?" she asked incredulously.

"I was taking care of business," Eric said snidely. That put Jessica over the edge. The shock, horror and disgust that she felt would easily get her off on temporary insanity in any court of law. Without even thinking, or knowing what she was doing, she grabbed a lead pipe from the floor. Tommy was still lifting and closing the lid, whining 'HELP ME'.

"You don't understand. It's not like that. Let me explain. The severed heads of mom and dad are fak..."

He was unable to finish the last word as the lead pipe came crashing down on his head.

Jessica was enraged. "Taking care of business? Taking care of business?"

She swung the pipe, accentuating each word, crushing his skull.

"TAKING. WHAAP CARE WHAAP OF WHAAP BUSINESS!" WHAAP.

Eric dropped to the floor from the first hit, without a struggle. Jessica stood over him, swinging the pipe over and over again, leaving a pool of blood, bones, and brains on the floor.

She stopped, breathing heavily; with her heart beating so fast, that it seemed like it would come right out of her chest.

She looked around, becoming fully cognizant of her surroundings. She walked over to the severed head of her mother that lay in the corner.

"That's odd. How come there isn't any blood?"

She picked up the head. Something wasn't right. It seemed fake. Unlike her shrunken boyfriend, who felt warm when she touched him, this seemed strangely cold. Now completely terrified, and confused, Jessica walked over to the shrunken Tommy. The lid was opening once again. She saw Tommy's face.

"Did he just blink?"

She felt his neck. A pulse was present.

"HELP ME," and the lid closed again.

Jessica felt paralyzed; frozen in time. A noise from the other side of the room brought her back to reality. A clear jar containing a dead cat swimming in formaldehyde came crashing to the ground. She looked to see what happened. Her mother and father's heads were staring at her in horror from the floor. This was way too much for Jessica to handle.

"Stay right here," she said to the shrunken version of Tommy. She began laughing at how ridiculous that statement was.

"Where the hell can you possibly go?" she crazily laughed.

She walked over, and picked up her father's head. He had the same facial expression as Donald Sutherland had in the final scene of the much better remake of 'Invasion of the Body Snatchers'.

"This is odd," she said, still in a state of shock. "Why does it feel so fake? Where is all of the blood?"
She squeezed the head. "HOLY SHIT! This isn't real. It's made of foam."
Jessica looked over to her boyfriend. The VERY REAL Tommy continued lifting up, and closing the lid on his new home. "HELP ME! HELP ME!"
Not completely understanding what was happening, she dropped the fake head, and picked up her mother's head. Squeezing it, she said in exasperation, "Another fake. What the fuck?!"
She looked over to her dead brother, laying on the floor in a pool of blood, compliments of a lead pipe. Looking back and forth from the real shrunken Tommy, to the fake foam heads of her parents, Jessica stood in shock and horror, drenched in blood. She heard a noise upstairs.
"Eric. Jessica. We're home."

11

It was her parents. Not knowing what to do, Jessica stood where she was, barely breathing. She could hear her parents walking throughout the house yelling their children's names.

"Eric. I know you were pissed off at us because your mother and I made last minute plans, causing you to cancel yours. I hope you told your sister that we weren't coming home last night. I know you really didn't mean it when you said that it would be better off if we were dead," said Mr. Peterson.

"Come on, honey. We're not mad anymore. I hate the way we left off last night," added Mrs. Peterson.

Jessica listened to all of this in a shocked silence, staring at her recently murdered brother, her shrunken boyfriend, and the blood that was dripping off of her onto the basement floor.

The conversation between her parents continued.

"She's not upstairs," said Mrs. Peterson. "If she's with Tommy, why are both his car and her car in the driveway?"

"I'm not sure about that", said Mr. Peterson. One thing that I am willing to bet you on, is that we can find Eric downstairs. Knowing him, he's most likely plotting our death," he laughed to himself.

A new level of horror struck Jessica with that last comment. Unfortunately, it was too late. The door to the basement opened.

Mrs. Peterson gasped at the sight. Mr. Peterson blurted out, "What in Holy Hell happened?"

There stood Jessica at the bottom of the stairs, her Evil Dead shirt drenched in blood, as Eric's lifeless body lie on the floor, oozing blood, bones and brain. Thin Lizzy's 'Jailbreak' ended. The CD changer began playing the next track from Eric's Classic Rock selection. Randy Bachman's 1974 anthem, 'Takin' Care of Business' began playing, as Mr. and Mrs. Peterson went downstairs looking for answers.

THE END

THE DARK SECRET

On a dark, desolate road the car came to an abrupt stop. I was fumbling with my phone to see how many likes my latest FaceBook post received.

"75 Likes for a picture of me posing at a local Rite Aid?" I asked out loud to no one in particular. "It has to be the suit!"

It was at that moment that I looked up and noticed the brake lights from the car in front of me. I swerved to the left, just in time to avoid a collision. My first thought was that I needed to get a look at this asshole. I sped up on his left, laughing as I drove past this person, proudly displaying my middle finger. I made sure the interior light was on, so the driver could see my finger in its Full Glory!

It reminded me of the old George Carlin joke: 'Did you ever notice that anyone driving slower than you is an asshole, and anyone driving faster is a maniac'? I guess if he were alive today he would need to add a third part: Anyone driving while texting is a douchebag!

As I drove by waving my digitus medius manaically, a strange thought hit me: this asshole looked exactly like my father. With the timing of a bad horror movie, my phone began to ring, breaking the silence, causing me to jump. I set it to bluetooth, and answered the phone.

"Hey, mom. How are you?"

"Well, hello my # 1 son," she answered.

"The ONLY reason you say that is because I am your only son," I shot back.

She laughed, and added, "Don't forget that tomorrow is your father's birthday."

I'm hurt that you think I would forget something as important as that," I lied as I muttered' Oh Shit' to myself. I need to buy a present!

My mother continued. "Harold rented a hall, and wants to throw him a big bash for his 70th Birthday."

"Great. When is this epic party taking place?"

"He called in some favors, and he will be renting The VFW in Watertown tomorrow night from 6pm-3am."

I know Harold is dad's best friend, but you have to admit that he is one impulsive prick! I mean, he's lucky that I don't have plans. A little notice would have been nice!"

I heard a sigh on the other end, which was code for stop being so negative.

I let out a breath and said, "Mom. I can't wait. It's going to be a great time! The best part will be watching dad's expression as he opens my gift."

"Richard, don't tell me that you didn't get a gift yet?"

"Alright, I won't tell you. But I do have to go," I lied. Before my mother could respond, I said, "I love you", and clicked the stop button on my steering wheel, disconnecting my call.

"SHIT! SHIT! SHIT!" I screamed, as my fist pounded the steering wheel, each time more forcefully. "What the hell am I going to get him???!!!"

2

At that exact moment, the car driven by my dad's doppleganger seemed to think that I was driving too slow for him, and decided to pass me on the left. Normally I would mind my own business, and continue driving. Road Rage now is much more violent than it was back in the 70's. Back then, the worst might result in a yelling match before both drivers drove away thinking the other was in the wrong. Now, forget about it. I have heard stories of people being stabbed or shot over a dirty look. This time was different. Maybe it was my adrenaline talking, but something just didn't seem right, and I wanted to stay and find out. It was 10:30pm on a dark road, without any streetlights, and there were only a couple of houses. What would a visitor be doing here this late at night? An elderly couple lived in this neighborhood. They reminded me of the grandparents from Willy Wonka. The Gene Wilder version, not the Johnny Depp remake.

"I hope he doesn't plan on stopping there. The only thing that would keep them up this late is a good old-fashioned 'Matlock' Marathon!!!"

I chuckled to myself as I made a U-Turn. I was now facing the other car, on the other side of the road. A large tree in the front yard of the house I was next to kept me hidden. Ensuring that my headlights were off, and I was unable to be seen, I now waited to see how these events were going to unfold.

I watched and waited as my father's doppleganger sat in his car staring at the house he was now parked in front of, for what seemed like an eternity. In reality, it was only 5 minutes. He sat and stared for another 10 minutes. I began to nod off, and would have succeeded if it wasn't for the buzzing emanating from my back pocket.

"This damn phone, "I muttered to no one in particular.

I ignored it, fearing that the light would bring me unwanted attention from the mystery driver. Just as the buzzing stopped, I heard the car door open.

"Ahhhh. Finally!!! Now this should become interesting."

The mystery driver stepped out of the car, seeming overly cautious for someone that is supposed to be there. He walked to the back of the car, fished in his pocket for what appeared to be his keys, and proceeded to open the trunk using the key.

"What the hell? Is this 1977? Who opens a trunk manually? This is one weird dude!"

I began to hum the dueling banjos theme from 'Deliverance'.

Once the trunk was open, he jammed his hand back into his pocket, searching furiously for something. Even in the darkness, I was able to sense his anger and frustration as his hands went from his front pockets to his back pockets, to the front once again.

He muttered incoherently to himself, as he forcefully threw the junk found in his pockets to the ground, allowing his hands to go even deeper, hoping that he would miraculously find what he needed. He plunged into his left front pocket one more time, and this time I saw him pull out a small object. It was too dark to see what it was, but when I saw him squeeze the two sides and it lit up, I realized that it was a small flashlight.

"This guy is Old School. First he opens his trunk manually, now he needs a flashlight to examine his trunk. I wouldn't be surprised if he rolled his windows up by hand."

What I thought was going to be a somewhat boring evening, was quickly turning into a very interesting night.I began to feel like the love-child of Columbo and Angela Lansbury. The thought of my two favorite television detectives from the 80's getting it on made me both laugh and cringe at the same time.

"Hey. Maybe I was the love child of Baretta and Police Woman Angie Dickinson. That at least, made more sense!"

As I began turning all of my favorite detective shows into one big orgy, I almost forgot where I was, and what I was doing. The slamming of the trunk snapped me out of it.

I looked up to see him staring intently at the house in a strange and creepy way.

"What is this dude's major malfunction?"

He looked at his watch, sighed, and walked to the driver's side door. He reached his arm through the open window, leaned in, and began to lay on the horn. No movement, or lights turned on in the house. He pressed down on the horn even harder, as if this would make it louder. Still nothing. Now he seemed even more agitated. He laid on the horn a third time.

"Why don't you call him on his cell, you backwards motherfucker. Let me guess. You only have a landline?!"

The third time was the charm, as I saw a light emanate from one of the rooms. The porchlight then went on, and the front door opened. Out came a short, overweight man with a receding hairline. A bad combover was not fooling anyone. He looked to be in his mid-thirties. He squinted at the dark form in the road.

"This street could really use some streetlights," I thought.

The portly gentleman took one step onto the porch to get a better look. I could see the look of recognition on his face.

He went to the door, and yelled into the house, "It's alright honey. It's only the Uber Driver."

He lifted up his forefinger, giving the universal sign for, 'I'll be there in a minute'. He walked inside, grabbed his phone, a small briefcase, and started walking toward the driver.

"Aren't you going to say goodbye?" A beautiful looking woman with long blonde hair and a slender build walked out to give him a kiss.

"Be careful honey, " she continued.

"Come on, Beth. It's only a bachelor party, and I don't have to drive, thanks to this Modern Marvel known as Uber. What could possibly go wrong?" he shot back.

I'm not naive Norman. I know how you and your friends get after a few drinks. Hennessy and Uber are the reasons why we have 3 kids," she joked as he began walking towards the car.

"Come on honey. You know I'm a changed man. I'm not the same 25 year old kid you met at a Pearl Jam concert," he said as he grabbed her ass.

Hey!. What are you doing? The Uber driver can see you. I'm a lady!" she exclaimed as she grabbed his crotch.

"Oooh, baby. That's how I like it!"

Beth squeezed it even harder, and said, "If you want to continue liking it, then you better keep it in here! Now have a great, no correction, OK time tonight"

"Oh, honey. You know you're the only one for me," he said as he got down on one knee in full proposal mode.

"I love you too, Normie"

I stuck my finger in my mouth as in a mock gag and said, "This is by far the worst Lifetime Movie I have ever seen!"

Norm approached the car. The driver ripped the briefcase out of his hand without saying a word, and walked it to the open trunk.

Norm seemed startled by the abruptness.

"I'm guessing they didn't hire you for your Customer Service skills," he said sarcastically.

Still no reaction. Norm was determined to draw out a response. He continued," You came in the nick of time. My wife was on the verge of castrating me!"

Norm grabbed his shoulder, pulling him to face him, saying, "Come on bud. If we're not going to be friends, the least we can do is be cordial."

This finally elicited a response. The driver pushed his hand away forcefully, driving Norm off-balance as he almost fell backwards.

What an asshole!" I said out loud to myself, as I continued watching the show from across the street. As Norm regained his balance, the driver threw the briefcase in the trunk and slammed it shut. Norm was about to say, 'Hey, be careful with that', but never had a chance. The driver walked to the passenger door, opened it, went to the front door, opened that door, got in, and started the car, still not saying a single word.

A feeling of nervousness prevented Norm from saying what he really wanted to say. He was never one for confrontation. His mouth opened as if he was going to give him a piece of his mind. Instead, he got in the backseat, and closed the door.

"Hey, boss. What is your name?"

The driver turned around, gave him a dead stare without speaking, and pressed on the gas while the car was idling in neutral

"Well, I guess I'm not paying you for your witty repartee," Norm said, trying to relieve the tension. "Do you have the address?"

Without saying a word, the driver typed an address into his phone, which was acting as a GPS.

Now Norm was becoming annoyed. "With your winning personality, I know what to call you. Mike, as in Michael Myers." Now he was becoming cocky. "Come on Mike, take me to the party," he said, as he slapped 'Mike' on the shoulder.

Mike, still stone-faced and silent, gave him a dirty look.

"Alright, alright," Norm said as he put both arms up as in surrender.

I was surprised at how well the sound carried, and that I was able to eavesdrop on the entire conversation.

I thought good ole Normie gave the driver too much credit by naming him after my favorite movie killer, Michael Myers.

"The boogeyman has much more personality than this asshole! He reminds me of Terry Schiavo.......AFTER the coma!!!"

3

Just then, Mike put the car in drive and sped down the street. I started my car, and said, "Let's go and see how this wacky night is going to end." I put my car in drive, and began to follow. In the pit of my stomach, I had a very bad feeling that it wasn't going to end well.

I was following the car several car lengths behind, not wanting to give myself away, when a minor panic attack struck: it's after 11pm, and I still haven't picked up a gift for my father. It only lasted several seconds when I remembered that it's not 1983, and I could buy a gift online anytime. That thought made me laugh. I turned on the radio to my favorite station on satellite radio:'70's on 7'. I continued to follow, humming along to 'Take The Money and Run'. By now I was becoming bored and hungry. I realized I was getting closer, and he might realize that I am following. By this time, I stopped caring. An empty stomach, along with apathy, will do that to you.

"Fuck this!" I said, as I put on my blinker and turned left onto a side street.

Just as I was turning, I saw the brake lights on 'Mike's' car, as he pulled over on the side of the road. I immediately pulled over, looking through the rearview mirror.

He turned the car off, got out, and began walking to the back of the car. I stepped out of my car, closed the door quietly, and conveniently placed myself behind a tree in the yard closest to the road.

"Why the hell did we stop?" asked Norman from the backseat.

Mike opened the trunk without a reply. He grabbed something small and shiny, and closed the trunk. Highly agitated, Norm opened his door, and stepped out.

"Are you an Uber driver, or Marcel Marceau? I could have a better conversation with Helen Keller!"

As Norm was walking to the back of the car, screaming into the night air, I saw 'Mike' drop the small, shiny object on the ground. If my detective skills were accurate, and how can they not be, seeing that I am the love-child of famed 70's tv dectectives, it seemed deliberate.

By now, Norm was livid. He got into the drivers face, saying loudly, "Now can you understand me? Does this help? He was miming fake sign language as he said this.

Mr Uber was unfazed. He didn't even flinch. I hated to admit that I was impressed. Norm was livid. He just stood staring at him, not sure what to say next. Mike pointed to the ground, where he had dropped the object.

"Oh, is that it? You want me to pick that up for you? If I get this, then can you finally take me to where I am I am paying you to take me?"

He waited a second for a response, and said, "Why am I even bothering talking? It's obvious the 'Pinball Wizard' cannot, or will not, respond."

'I have to say Norm seems like a spoiled, arrogant asshole, but his references to 1970's pop culture was amusing,' I thought to myself.

Norm was now all on fours, searching for this unknown object. Meanwhile, I saw the driver dig his hand deep into his pocket. I couldn't see what it was, but it was small, and had a shimmer to it.

"Damn! I wish there was some kind of lighting. I can't see shit," exclaimed Norm as his hands searched blindly for the unknown object. I saw him grab something. He stood up, and attempted to hand the object over.

"Is this what was so important to you? Can we go now?"

At that moment, Michael lunged at Norm with his left hand.

"What the fuck was that?" Norm said, confused and scared, reaching down to his abdomen.

The driver lunged again and again and again. It took me several seconds to realize that what he had was a knife, and Norm was being stabbed repeatedly. I stood hidden (I hoped) behind the tree, paralyzed with fear. I saw Norm writhing around, screaming in pain. One last stab to the kidneys silenced him for good. Norm's body shook violently one last time, and then everything fell quiet. Blood began to trickle out of his mouth.

The driver, still standing over him, wiped the blade on his pants, looked around to see if there were any witnesses he would have to 'take care of', and then put the blade back in his pocket. Unfortunately for Norm, there wasn't a single house within a 5 mile radius. His head peering around in every direction, now appeared to be looking directly at me. My sphincter tightened with fear. I stayed perfectly still, I even stopped breathing. Feeling confident that no one saw him, he walked over to the body and attempted to pick it up. Mike struggled lifting the body. It seems that Norm's extra weight was too much for him. He dropped him on the ground. Muttering incoherently, he picked up the body a second time. The top half of his body hit the pavement hard, crushing the left side of his face. Mike dragged him by the feet to the trunk. He lifted the body into the trunk, and tried to close it. Norm's head was not all the way in. The trunk came crashing down on his skull. Brain fragments, along with small pieces of bone, oozed onto the street.

I let out a sigh of relief while this was happening. I developed a small cramp in my left leg. Several years ago I damaged that leg exercising to the 'INSANITY' DVD. I had since stopped my exercising, but the damage had been done. As he was awkwardly putting the corpse into the trunk, I slipped into my unseen car to relieve the pressure.

Mike, as I was now calling him, pulled the trunk down once again with all his strength. The skull was crushed even more. This time Norm's eyeball became detached from its retina, hanging by what looked like a long string. He did it one more time, for his own amusement, before pushing the body completely in the trunk and walking to the driver's side.

"What a sick fuck!" I said quietly to myself, stretching my leg, trying to ease the cramp.

Mike started the car.

"Thank God!" I started to laugh, one part nerves, the other at the irony. "Here I am talking to God once again. At least this time I am thanking HIM!"

Just as I thought I was in the clear, I felt the start of a large spasm develop. Without any control, my leg kicked up, and hit the hazard lights. The horn was going off uncontrollably, and the lights lit up the entire street.

"Oh Fuck!"

4

Mike turned his attention to me, just as I was sitting up to alleviate the pain. This time there was no mistake about it. He was staring directly at me. Our eyes met. With the hazard lights blinking on and off furiously, I could now see his face, and what scared me the most: his eyes. They seemed lifeless, as cold as a shark. He gave me the look of death, mixed with confusion and anger. I could sense that he was processing everything that was happening, and even scarier, what he needed to do next.

He reached into his pocket, pulled out what I now knew was the knife, and began to walk towards my car. I grabbed hold of the steering wheel to help pull myself up into the driver's seat. My leg was still in full spasm mode, and the hazards were blinking like a Pink Floyd Laser Light Show. I heaved myself into the seat with a thunderous "FUUUUCK" , as my leg decided not to have any mercy. I looked up. Mad Mike was only 20 feet away. I reached into my pocket to grab the keys. NOTHING!

"Shit! I must have dropped them by the tree."

I began feeling underneath the seat furiously and blindly, hoping for some kind of miracle. He was now closer to 10 feet. I searched again hoping for a Hail Mary. Still nothing. I now realized that the window was open, and could only be closed with the car started. Oh, how I wish I could close them manually.

Frantically, I searched one more time.
"YESSSS!!!!"
I found them underneath the seat. I nervously flipped through the keys, looking for the one that started the car. Too late. I felt a slight breeze, and then a sharp pain in my shoulder, followed by a warm feeling of numbness. It wasn't until I saw the trickle of blood flowing down my arm, and onto the seat, that I realized that I had been stabbed. His arm raised again to begin stab # 2. He must have hit a nerve, because my fingers were now completely numb, preventing me from putting the window up. It was one of those moments that you don't know what you are capable of until you are actually in the moment. Without thinking, I opened the door with both hands, slamming it into Mike. This caught him off-guard, and knocked him to the ground. He appeared dazed, but I think it was more from the shock, than the actual pain. I went back to blindly searching for the correct key, unable to take my eyes off this killer that eerily resembled my dad. I found the key, jamming it into the starter. My aim was off, and the keys once again ended up on the floor. I watched as he sat up, checking out his surroundings. It was a scene directly out of my favorite horror movie, 'Halloween'.
"Sorry Mike, not this time."

I picked up the key, and put it into the starter. It didn't turn over. Mike regained his senses, and stood up. He looked at me, and began to dust himself off. I turned the key again. It made some noises that told me it wanted to turn over. Mike, moving slower , and a bit more cautious, began walking to the car with knife in hand.

"Come on you piece of shit. START!"

As if on cue, my car started, and I quickly put it into drive. Feeling confident (maybe a little too much) now, I flipped him off, and screamed, "I don't think so. Maybe some other time, you low-life piece of shit!"

5

As I drove down the dark, desolate road, I could see him running to his car in my rearview mirror. I hit the gas even harder, accelerating my speed to 65 miles per hour, then 70, now 85 mph. I glanced once again in my rearview mirror. The headlights were becoming smaller and smaller as I increased the distance between me and the psychopath.

I finally began to relax a bit. Unfortunately, that is when the pain in my shoulder began to throb. I was losing blood, but luckily the cut wasn't that deep. That didn't stop the pain from increasing. I began searching the car for something that could help stop the bleeding. On the passenger side floor, I saw five or six Dunkin Donuts napkins. D&D was always my first stop on my way to work in the morning, and no matter if it was a bagel, or a cup of coffee, they would always give me several napkins with my purchase. My attempt to reach them while I was driving was futile. I knew that I must pull over.

I looked once again in the rearview mirror to ensure that dad's doppleganger was not following me. Nothing but darkness! Feeling much more comfortable with the situation, I slowed my car to a crawl, and parked on the side of the road. I put the car in park, and turned off my headlights.

Using the inside light, I reached for the napkins. Without much thought I pulled my blood splattered shirt over my head. I had to stop one it reached my shoulders.

The pain was unbearable. I took several deep breaths, and tried again.

I let out a loud scream, and stopped again. At that moment, the voice of my mother spoke to me just like when I was 5 years old, and I scraped my knee. "Come on, Richie. It's like ripping off a bandaid. Just tear it off as fast as you can without thinking."

"She's right!" I said out loud. "Stop being such a pussy!"

That 'Full Metal Jacket' mentality worked as I attempted to rip the shirt over my shoulders and head in one quick motion. I'm impressed that my screams didn't shatter any windows. I twisted my body to make it easier to tear off. I wanted to stop, but knew that I couldn't. I got it as far as my neck, when the shirt became tangled. I struggled some more, twisting and turning.

I yanked one last time, screaming until the shirt was off. I realized that using the D&D napkins was useless. I rolled the shirt into a ball, and placed it on the wound, and pressed down hard, hoping I could curtail the bleeding. My platelets kicked in, and most of the blood had conjealed into blobs.

The shirt now looked like a used tampon. I threw it into the back seat. It was then that I remembered I had a t-shirt in my trunk given to me at a recent radio promotion. I won it answering trivia questions. It was 3 sizes too big for me, and I never had any intention of wearing it. Hell, I didn't even like that station. Now, I was happy I kept it.

I opened my door, and walked to the trunk.
A gust of wind picked up, causing more pain to the
wound.
I opened the trunk and began searching for my 106.9
WCCC t-shirt. It was underneath some junk that
began piling up. Without hesitation, I slipped on my
oversized shirt, once again causing so much pain
that my eyes began to water. I bit down on my
tongue to keep myself from screaming.
Just as I was closing the trunk, a pair of headlights
appeared from behind me. The fear stopped me in
my tracks. I was unable to see what kind of car it
was, but it was going unusually fast, and appeared to
be gaining speed.
"FUCK! I'M DEAD!"

6

I slammed the trunk shut, and reached into my back pocket for my cellphone.

"Mike, daddy's doppleganger, asshole, whatever your name is, your days of killing are over!" I blurted out with a somewhat maniacal laugh.

I was about to dial the police when I noticed that I had 14 LIKES on a recent FaceBook Post. I'm not sure if it was the loss of blood, or the stress from the terror I was enduring, but something snapped me out of it.

"I have a homicidal maniac coming towards me, and I'm worried about my FB post?" I said to myself, realizing how ludicrous it was that it would even be a concern at this moment.

"What the hell am I thinking? If I don't call the police now, my next post will be informing everyone about my funeral arrangements!"

Just as reality hit me in the face like a ton of bricks, my screen flickered. I saw that my phone only had 2% life left.

"SHIT! I forgot to charge it!"

I scrambled to get to the phone app and began dialing 911. I dialed 9. The phone flickered. I dialed 1. It flickered again. The car was now racing faster, coming straight at me. I went to dial the final 1. A woman picked up.

"Waterbury Police Depar........." The phone died. In a fit of rage, I threw the phone on the ground, smashing it.

The car was now at my side.

7

"Get out of the middle of the road, asshole!"
screamed a drunken teenager, as the car screamed
past me. Not before his drunken buddy threw a half
empty Budweiser can at me. The can hit me square
in the chest, and then rolled to the side of the road,
stopping at the curb. My fresh t shirt now smelled
like stale beer. Any other day, this would have sent
me off on an obscenity- laced tirade, but all I did
now was laugh with relief.

I stood there in shock for a second as many thoughts
went through my head:

1)I need to get the hell out of here
2)I need a new phone
3)I need to call the police
4)I need to get myself to an emergency room

All of these thoughts continued to race through my
head ,as I jumped in the car, driving full speed ahead.

8

Meanwhile 10 miles behind, 'Mike' was feeling a bit groggy from the hit to his head.He was now driving aimlessly, looking lost. He glanced at his GPS, and took a right onto a side street. This area was lighted, and had many more houses than his previous stop. He saw a small Victorian house on his left, and began to slow down. He pulled to the side of the road, stopped the car, and was just about to lay on the horn, until he looked in his rearview mirror. He noticed dried blood caked above his left eyebrow. He opened the glove compartment, found a slightly soiled napkin, spat on it, and began to wipe the blood off. Mike turned on the interior light to get a better look, searching for cuts, bruises or scratches. When he was content that he had cleaned himself up well enough that no questions would be asked, he laid on the horn, waiting for his next stop to come to the car.

The porch light was on, and three loud, drunken twenty somethings came bursting out of the door.

"Thank God for Uber," said one of the men.

"No, more like 'Thank God for Nick's credit card!" exclaimed the second man, holding up the credit card, and laughing hysterically.

"What was that about my credit card?" said an obviously annoyed Nick.

"Why are you looking at me? I didn't say anything."

Nick looked to his other friend, who had just finished jamming the credit card into his back pocket.

"Don't look at me either. I've got morals!" he said holding his chin up high in mock pride.

"Yeah, said Nick. Last time, your so-called morals cost me $400 on a boat rental."

"You have to admit, we did have a great time."

That may be true, but I can't be supporting you two bums my whole life!"

Attempting to change the subject, and more importantly, getting Nick to talk about something else, the other friend, whose name was Clay blurted out, "Hey, what party are we off to now?"

"Oh, you're going to love this, Romeo," Nick said to Clay. "We are off to Jacquelyn's house."

Nick knew all about the crush that Clay had on Jacquelyn. In fact, everyone did.

"With all of the alcohol flying, Nick said to Clay, she might actually find you somewhat human for a couple of hours."

"OOOOH YEAH!" said the friend that was paying for Uber with Nick's credit card. His name was Tom.

"Clay's about to see his one true love!"

"Shut the fuck up! said Clay, as he playfully pushed Tom.

"Come on, said Nick. Will you girls stop fighting for at least 3 seconds? Let's have some fun!"

The three men walked down to the parked car. Mike opened his door to let himself out.

"Hey, Nick. I hope you remembered the suitcase at the bottom of the stairs. I have a feeling that if everything goes as planned, I will need a change of clothes in the morning," said an overly excited and over confident Clay.

"First of all, you don't need to scream. I'm right here! Second of all, it's right here asshole," as he threw the baggage on the road directly in front of the trunk.

"Hey, Senor, said Tom. Will you open up the trunk for us. We have a suitcase that needs to go in there." Mike glared at them without speaking.

"Well are you going to open the trunk or what?" asked Nick.

Mike continued to stare quietly for another 3-5 seconds, before saying that the latch was broken, and they would have to bring the suitcase with them in the backseat.

"You gotta be fucking kidding me," said Tom. We're stuck with a broken down Uber. I demand a discount!"

Mike didn't say a word. He continued with his icy stare, while opening up the back door for them to get in.

"You must pride yourself on your customer service skills," Tom said, as the three of them laughed, getting into the car.

I know you have the address to Jacquelyn's love hut in your GPS, or is that broken as well?"

Mike didn't bother with a response. Instead, he just started the car, and put it into drive.

The car bucked somewhat as he put it into third gear.

"Jesus! Where the hell did you learn to drive?" exclaimed Thomas, as he was thrown forward, and then back, causing a sharp pain in his neck.

Ignoring his belligerent passengers, Mike continued to drive. He glanced at his GPS, and realized a sharp left was coming up. He turned the wheel all the way to the left, causing everyone in the car to fall to the right. The body in the trunk also moved, causing a loud THUNK sound.

"Hey, did you hear that? asked Clay.

"Hear what?" asked Thomas.

"I'm not sure, but I think I heard something heavy moving in the trunk.

"I thought you said the latch was broken?" Clay said in a condescending tone, pushing the driver with his hand.

"What's back there? An ex girlfriend?" he asked, pushing him once again.

Clay was nonstop with his taunting.

"Hey, Norman Bates. Mom wants out of the trunk, pushing him a third time.

Mike didn't even flinch, but after being pushed, his foot pressed harder on the accelerator. The speed went from 35-40, up to 60 mph. By this time, the boys were much more aware of their safety.

"What the fuck are you doing? This isn't The Daytona 500!" said Nick, trying his best to sound normal, but the tone of fear and concern was noticeable.

Mike pressed on the pedal even harder. First 60, then 70, now 75 miles per hour, on the somewhat lighted street. Just then a deer ran out of the woods, and into the direct path of the vehicle.

"HOLY FUCK!" screamed Clay, as he pushed Mike once again.

Mike swerved to the left, nearly missing the deer. This caused him to hit a pothole. The car went down, then up, causing the three men to hit their head on the ceiling. The body in the trunk was being thrown around like a rodeo clown.

"That time I definitely heard it!" yelled Thomas.

What the hell is going on?" Nick yelled.

Mike , ignoring their questions, turned the radio on. He took a hard right turn, hitting a smaller pothole. The body in the trunk made another loud THUNK. The boy's concerns were drowned out by Mike turning up the volume on his radio. Nick attempted to scream over the deafening guitars of Megadeth to no avail.

"LET US OUT, YOU MACMURPHY MOTHERFUCKER!" screamed Nick, referring to Jack Nicholson's character in the classic. 'One Flew Over The Cukoo's Nest'.

He threatened to open his passenger door. Clay reached out the open window and lifted the door handle.

This caused the indoor light to go on. Mike turned his body around in a frenzy to stop the madness that he created.

The sound of a siren, and the red and blue lights turning, woke up the dark road. Hidden in a small clearing on the side of the road, a police cruiser pulled behind the car, requesting it to pull over. Mike hesitantly pulled the car to the curb, and waited. There was a lot of nervous chatter coming from the back seat.

9

"Let's get the hell out of here!" pleaded Clay, as he opened the side door.

The police officer was now walking to the right side, shining his light into the car.

"Going anywhere?" asked the officer in a slightly sarcastic tone.

Clay was just about to speak, when Nick spread his right arm across his chest, pushing Clay back in his seat.

"No officer, said Nick. We are just getting a ride from this Uber driver.

The officer shining his light in and around the car,was now walking towards the drivers side.

"Be cool man. Be Cool," whispered Nick.

Clay began to protest, but calmed down when the officer walked up to Mike, shining his flashlight in his face.

"Is that right Mr. Uber driver? I'd like to see some ID."

Mike reached into his back pocket, grabbed his wallet, and gave the officer his license.

"Thank you sir. Now just sit tight while I run your plates."

The officer walked back to the cruiser.

"Shit! We have to tell him about the trunk," said Thomas. "You heard it. You know you did!" he said, looking both left to right, from Nick to Clay.

"What the hell are we going to say?

Hey, I think our Uber driver killed his mama, and is now having her ride first class in the trunk."

"Works for me!" answered Thomas.

Clay was unusually quiet, as the other two debated back and forth. He began wiping away at a small red spot on the front passenger side. It seemed somewhat fresh, and had a weird copper smell to it. He licked his finger, and rubbed the spot again with his forefinger.

"What the hell are you doing?" asked Nick.

The driver was acting very calm. Almost too calm. It was eerie.

"I'm not sure, but I think that's blood!"

All three began staring at the spot, when they were suddenly jolted back to reality by the officer walking back to the driver's side door.

"I checked it out. You're all set. Do me a favor, and slow down. You wouldn't want someone driving like a psycho with your kids being put in harms way."

"Officer! Officer!" said Clay, as he attempted to scream out the passenger side window.

Mike put his license away, and started the car.

"Officer, I need to tell you something!"

Clay's voice was drowned out by the revving of the automobile. Mike turned the radio up once again, drowning out Clay.

"Officer, I need to......."

His voice was a distant blur, as Mike began driving down the road.

He turned the radio even louder. The three boys looked at each other in a fearful way, wondering if they were in a car with one weird dude, or a potential killer.

10

I was still speeding down the road in complete fear.
My car had not gone under 65 mph in 20 minutes. It
was like a bad remake of the movie 'Speed'. I
chuckled to myself at that thought, because
NOTHING could be as bad as the original!.
My shoulder was still throbbing. I knew I had to stop
somewhere soon to purchase a first aid kit, along
with a charger to get my phone working. I was
pissed that my anger allowed me to smash it on the
road, but was happy that I regained my senses in
time to pick it back up, and bring it with me. The
screen was cracked in several areas, but it didn't
appear broken. I felt lost not being able to use my
phone as a GPS. I glanced in the rearview mirror.
NOTHING!! I suddenly began to calm down, and
eased my foot on the gas. As I slowed, I passed my
first road sign. It read: Next Exit 5 miles: Food, Gas,
and Restrooms. The anticipation of cleaning my
wound, and calling the police on my daddy
doppleganger, Uber Psycho Killer 'Friend' caused me
to speed up once again. A yellow light appeared on
the dashboard, indicating that I was extremely low
on gas.
"Talk about a ClusterFuck of a night!"
I drove the 5 miles, got off at the exit, taking a right,
following the signs to gas, and hopefully a pharmacy.
I noticed a small gas station on my left. I turned into
the lot.

"What a shithole!"

The parking lot light was on, but all of the pumps were closed, and the station was completely dark. CLOSED FOR RENOVATION read the sign.

"Of course it is!" I mocked, as I pulled back onto the road.

Just as I was pulling out into the road, the squealing of brakes kicked my reflexes back into action, as I backed up just in time. A car going at an unbelievably dangerous speed nearly tore off my front bumper. As the car passed, a sense of familiarity kicked in. It only took a second to realize who and what it was. He slowed down just enough so that I could see who it was.

"The fucking Uber Driver!"

Did he actually smirk at me as he slowed down, or was it just my overactive imagination? What wasn't my imagination were what looked like 3 frat packers screaming in the backseat; correction:2. The person in the middle seemed to be just lying there as if asleep, possibly dead. I attempted to pull into traffic once again.

"Fuck my arm! I'm going to make this bastard pay myself!"

11

Before pulling out, I looked to my right to check for
traffic. The light had just turned green, which started
a barrage of cars coming my way. I backed up some
more, realizing that I was blocking part of the lane.
Due to my frustration, I hit the gas harder than I
intended, propelling me backwards until I heard a
loud BAM.

"FUUUUUCK!!" I screamed in total disgust.

I put the car in park, and walked to the back to
inspect the damage, and find out what the hell I hit. I
was unable to use the flashlight app on my phone
because of the dead battery, but luckily the parking
lot lights were ample. A broken taillight was the only
damage that I could see. I looked up to see what
could possibly be in the middle of a gas station
parking lot. A newspaper kiosk.

"A fucking kiosk!"

From the look of it, my bumper had smashed the
glass. A copy of the local paper had fallen out, and
was resting on my bumper. I picked it up, and was
just about to toss it, when the headline on the front
page caught my attention: Former Mental Patient
Eludes Authorities Once Again. It wasn't really the
headline that caught by attention, it was the picture
that accompanied it. I stared in disbelief, not
wanting to believe my own eyes.

It was my dad, or someone that was identical to him in every way. I walked to where the light was to get a better look. My hands were trembling as I began to read the article. Former mental patient Michael Zembruski has been on the run from authorities for the last several weeks. I couldn't believe what I was reading. He looked exactly like my father, had the same last name, and grew up in the same area. There was no way that all of this was a coincidence. The article continued to say that he was institutionalized at a young age by his parents. Years later, after he was deemed normal by doctors, he was sent to a halfway house where he could attempt to regain a normal life. Everything was fine for the next 5 years. He got his license, worked part time at a grocery store, and even made some friends. Suddenly, weird things, such as neighborhood pets disappearing, and blood found on his clothing, had doctors and caretakers asking questions. He was told he couldn't leave until the authorities were able to ask some questions. They never had a chance. He was gone the following morning, without a trace.

Thoughts raced through my head, causing me to ask myself many questions:

'Who the hell is this guy'?

'Why does he look exactly like my father'?

'Why does he have the same last name'?

242

12

Fear, rage, and anxiety overcame me. I needed to sit down in the car before I passed out. Calling my father to get some answers was just added to my already long list of things to get done tonight:

1) First Aid Kit

2)Fill my tank with gas

3)Buy a charger

4)Find the damn doppleganger, and take care of it 'Death Wish' style

It is going to be one hell of a night!!!!!

I started the car, and pulled onto the road. The signal of a red gas pump appeared on my dash, indicating that I needed to get gas immediately. I saw some lights in the distance, giving me hope.

"Come on. We need to make it!" I said, sounding like I was encouraging the car more than myself.

Another half mile went by, before reaching any signs of life. I drove by several small garages that were closed, a small, family-owned pastry shop closed, and an Urban Outfitters, of course closed at this hour.

"Did I just drop out of a time machine into 1966?!"

I looked ahead, seeing the familiar logo of CVS.

"Finally!"

I turned into the parking lot. All of the lights were on, but I found it odd that there wasn't much traffic in the lot. As I was parking, I did notice some movement inside the store.

I jumped out of the car, and ran to the automatic doors. NOTHING! I tried to pry the door open. NOTHING! By this time, I began to feel like Sean Penn's character in Oliver Stone's underrated classic, 'Wrong Turn'.

"Goddamn Murphy's Law!"

I was just about to leave when I heard a noise inside. I looked in to see a small Mexican man put a can of soup back on the shelf that had dropped. I began banging on the door. He was either ignoring me, or couldn't hear me from inside. I used both hands to bang on the door, as I screamed, "HEY!!!!"

I could see his head bopping, as if he was listening to music. I looked again, and could now see earbuds attached to a wire, coming out of his left ear, leading into his back pocket.

"Hey! Hey!" I continued screaming and banging on the doors.

After the fifth or sixth bang, I saw him look my way. He took out his I-Pod, and hit pause.

"Finally!"

A small overweight Mexican man with thick glasses came to the foyer and said slowly in broken English, "Sorry. We are closed."

"You have to help me!" I bellowed.

He tilted his head to the right, like a dog that couldn't quite understand what his owner was saying. He paused, then repeated," Sorry senor. We are closed."

He looked confused and frightened. It was then that I realized that he was looking at the dried blood that seeped through my shirt. A seemingly crazed man with blood on his shirt, screaming and banging. I would be afraid as well. Another person overheard us as he walked by. He stopped to ask what was happening. He was also of Mexican descent, but his English seemed much better. I did my best to calm down, and explain myself.

"Sorry sir. I didn't mean to upset anyone. I was involved in an accident."

I could see him staring at my shoulder, looking me up and down, but not saying a word.

I continued. "Actually, I was stabbed, which was NO ACCIDENT! I'm trying to explain to Pedro. Is that his name? That's what his name badge says."

I was talking a mile a minute due to my nerves, anxiety, and the constant throbbing in my shoulder.

"I was attempting to tell Pedro that I am in desperate need of bandages, gauze, and a phone cord charger. It's an emergency. I also am in dire need of gas."

"Sorry sir. My name is Miguel. Pedro doesn't speak much English. We are the cleaning crew. The store closed at 10pm."

I looked at my watch. It was now 10:45pm.

I could feel my anxiety increasing. "I don't know the area well. Can you tell me what is open, and where?" There is a convenience store, with a gas station 3 miles down the road. It's open 24 hours."

245

He was explaining something to Pedro. I didn't stay to find out what he was talking about. I rushed back to my car. The red light came on once I started the car, as if taunting me that I will soon run out of gas.

13

Back on the road, I was now driving like an 80 year old woman taking a Sunday drive through the country. It was sluglike, as my head scanned from left to right, not wanting to miss it. Several miles later, I saw a large neon sign that proudly displayed: Barrett's Convenience Store and Gas. OPEN 24 HOURS. I pulled to the first gas pump, swiped my card, and let it fill the tank as I ran to the entrance. The door opened faster than I expected, and hit me in the shoulder. I let out a loud scream. I looked up, expecting to explain myself, but my scream was drowned out by screaming and yelling coming from inside. I went in, and took an immediate right to avoid the scuffle. I don't need anymore trouble tonight.

"Give me the fucking money!"

"I told you I gave you everything I have."

"Don't fucking lie to me. I'll put a hole in your goddamn head!"

That's right. I picked the one store that was in the process of being robbed. I quickly, and quietly made my way to the back of the store. I looked up at the Aisle Headers.

"Ahh. First-Aid, Aisle 8."

I grabbed some bandages, gauze, and some neosporin. I heard it was good. How the hell should I know what works best for a stab wound.

The yelling became much louder.

"I'll kill everyone one in here. Now give me the fucking money!"

At this point, my anxiety was replaced by anger. After a night of being chased, stabbed, and having the back bumper destroyed, I was now completely unfazed. The only thing I needed now was a phone charger. Of course, that had to be up front by the registers, where all of the action was. Just as I thought it was a lost cause, I saw a tall, skinny man with a bad 70's mustache crouching in Aisle 2. He looked up at me, and put his finger to his lips, signaling the universal language for 'SHHH'. I froze in my spot, not sure of what he had in mind. The tall, skinny man stood up, unbeknownst to anyone else, grabbed the pot of coffee that was brewing on the counter not far from the registers, and walked swiftly and quietly to the man with the gun. Three people that were kneeling on the floor with their hands behind their neck, put their heads between their legs.

"Hey, Asshole!"

This startled everyone. I heard audible gasps as everyone looked in the direction of where the voice was coming from.

"I hope you like your coffee black!"

The man in the ski mask looked to his right. The pot of scolding hot coffee was thrown at his face. He screamed in pain.

The cashier, thinking quickly, grabbed the bat behind the register, and swung at his arm carrying the gun. The gun went flying out of his hand, as several people jumped on him. No one seemed to notice me, or care that I was there during all of this commotion. I grabbed the phone charger, and was just about to leave, when I noticed a box containing the latest I-Pod. I grabbed that as well, said "HAPPY BIRTHDAY, DAD," and made my way out the door, and back to the car.

14

I put the pump back in place, put the receipt in my pocket, and threw everything in the passenger seat. I grabbed the Neosporin, but my senses prevailed, and decided that the charger was more important than my pain. I grabbed the charger, and was unable to crack open the plastic container it was in. After my fifth attempt at opening the package, and using many of the words I hear my father say on a regular basis, I realized that I needed some help. I used my car keys to tear apart the container. I inserted the driver's key into the plastic, and made a small tear. I was then able to rip it in half with my hands. I started the car, grabbed the cracked phone from my back pocket, and plugged it in. I waited patiently for the Apple symbol to appear, signaling that I had power. NOTHING!!!

"Shit!"

I was becoming anxious, silently praying that I did not break the phone. 15 seconds went by. NOTHING. My stomach felt queasy. Finally, after 30 seconds, the Apple appeared.

My first thought was to call the police. I knew that it had to be done eventually, but I decided that calling my favorite cop, former 'Cop of the Year', my dad, seemed like the first logical step.

I needed some answers before I began spouting off like a mental patient to the authorities. Even though he was officially retired, he was still heavily involved in the community. More importantly, he could, no correction: HE NEEDED, to answer some questions regarding one former mental patient on the run that not only had the same last name, but also bore a striking resemblance to dear ole dad.

15

I pulled out of the parking lot, and began driving in the direction of my parents house. The phone was at 10%, which meant that I could now use it. As I went to pick up the phone, I saw the word ALERT scrolling across the screen, with the headline: MENTAL PATIENT.....

"Yeah, yeah, yeah!" I muttered.

I hit the phone app, and under favorites, hit the word Mom. Within in half a ring, my dad picked up the phone.

"Thank God you are alright. I've been trying to reach you!" He sounded frenetic, almost crazed.

I tried to alleviate the mood by saying sarcastically, "Well, hello to you too!"

Rich, this is not a laughing matter. I'm sure you heard about a certain mental patient on the run."

"As a matter of fact, I have. That's my reason for calling."

My father continued talking like I wasn't even there. "That psycho is your uncle."

That last statement hit me like a ton of bricks to the face. I interrupted him.

"W... Wa..... Wait dad. Dad. DAD!!!"

That last one got his attention. Before he could start again, I said, "What Uncle? I thought you were an only child."

By now he was beginning to calm down, and started to speak more coherently.

"We never mentioned it to you, because we didn't think you needed, no correction, we didn't think you should know. I have a twin brother."

I wanted to say something, but I couldn't get my mouth to form the words, so I just listened.

My father continued. "He was never right in the head. He didn't speak a word for the first 4 years of his life."

My thoughts went back to the nickname that I came up for him, Michael Myers, realizing how accurate I actually was. I felt a shiver go up my spine.

Dad's voice snapped me out of it.

"It started out small. He would take my toys, and pretend that he didn't know where they went. He continued this denial even after your grandmother found my toys under his bed. It later escalated to small animals. As you know, I grew up next to the small pond that your grandfather built. It was filled with wildlife of all kinds: frogs, snakes, fish, even muskrats. He thought it would be fun to walk around the pond with a wiffle ball bat, and repeatedly bash the heads of frogs in. Your grandparents did their best to keep an eye on him, and punish him. That just made him withdraw even more. The small conversations that he would initiate with people completely stopped altogether. Then came the disappearance of cats and dogs in the area. Most of the neighbors thought it was the coyotes, but I suspected something much more sinister.

When we were in our teens, me and Mike had separate rooms. Your uncle's door was always shut at night, and locked. No one bothered him. Even Grammy and Grampy seemed hesitant to knock on the door to see if he was alright. One night I got up to use the bathroom. I had to walk past Mike's room. I crept on my toes, in fear of waking someone. On my way back to my bedroom, the hallway was dark, and I didn't want to turn on any lights. I was silently passing my brothers room, when I tripped on something in the dark hallway. I wasn't sure what I had tripped on, but the pain shot up through my foot. I put my hand over my mouth to muffle my scream of 'OUCH'. I fell into my brothers bedroom door. It opened. The shock of seeing the door open made me forget all about the pain. I looked into the room to see if I could see anything. My eyes still had not adjusted to the darkness. I was about to close the door, when I saw the curtain covering the bedroom window billowing from the wind. I felt a chill, and realized that the window was open. Quietly, I walked into the room, whispering his name. NOTHING! 'Mike. Mike, are you there?' Still nothing. I went back to the door, closed it, and turned on the bedroom light. The sudden brightness shocked my dilated pupils. It took several seconds for them to adjust. I looked over to the bed. It was empty. I went to the window, reaching my body as far out as it would go to see if there was any sign of him.

I continued to listen, still trying to wrap my head around everything he was telling me. I finally broke my silence.

"What happened? Did he jump out the window?"

"No," my father answered. "His bedroom was in the basement. All he had to do was open the window, and step out."

Not wanting to drag this out anymore, I asked, "Did you find him? Did you tell Grammy and Grampy? What did my uncle (I'm not sure if I could ever get used to saying that), do?"

I gave out these rapid fire questions, hoping to get some answers.

My father continued. "I looked out the window. I saw him walking out of the woods, and into the backyard. Instead of causing a big scene at 1am, I turned off the lights, closed the bedroom door, and went back to bed like nothing had ever happened."

"But why the hell didn't you say anything, " I interjected.

"I thought at the time it would be best not to alert him that I knew anything. That way, I could monitor his activity, and find out what he was up to."

"That's sounds like you, dad. ALWAYS the cop. Even at 15 years old!"

My dad gave a small chuckle at that, and continued with the story. "I noticed the same activity for the next several days. Finally, I couldn't take it anymore. I had to find out what he was doing during his midnight excursions.

Next time he goes out, I am going to follow him.
I kept my television on low the next night, and
waited. The walls were thin, and I laid there patiently
in bed with my ear to the wall. It just turned 10pm
when I heard some rustling in the next room. I
laughed when the commercial on tv said, 'It's 10pm.
Do you know where your child is?'
Quietly, to myself, I answered, 'I'm about to find out!'
I looked out the bedroom window, and saw my
brother walking into the woods. My heart almost
stopped, as I saw him walking the family dog on a
leash into the woods. What made it even more
bizarre, and downright terrifying, was that he was
also carrying a huge wooden bat, and something
much smaller in his other hand.
I interrupted, "Not Angus?'
Angus was always dad's favorite pet growing up.
Everytime I bring up that name, he becomes quiet,
and his eyes well up with tears.
My father didn't say anything for several seconds. I
was about to ask if he was still there, when he
solemnly said, "Yes. It was Angus. I decided to give
him a 3 minute headstart before following. I didn't
want to scare him off, before finding out what he
was doing late at night in the woods. In hindsight, I
wish I had."
The only response to come out of my mouth was,
"Shit!"

I suspected what happened next. Did you stop him before he killed Angus. You never told me what happened to that dog, just that you didn't want to talk about it.

"I know. It kills me to even think about it. What happened next is that my fear and anxiety got the best of me. I ran down the stairs, leaving a loud CLOMPING sound on each step. Without thinking, I also slammed the door shut. Immediately, the lights went on in the house. It was your grandparents. I stopped, and was going back in to explain, when I heard a loud YELP coming from the woods. At this point, I turned around, running into the woods screaming, 'Mike! Mike!'

It was dark, and hard to see where I was going. I ran toward the loud cries of Angus, mixed with the low rumblings of Mike. I heard a loud WHAP. I ran faster. Another YELP. I could hear the voices of my parents calling my name from a distance. I didn't care. I kept running towards the screams. There was another loud WHAP, and then silence. I continued running, tripping on sticks, and the undergrowth in the woods. It would have been pitch black. Luckily, we had clear skies and a full moon shining the way. Up ahead, I saw the dark outline of my brother covering a hole.

"Mike, what the hell are you doing?"

What bothered me the most, and sent a chill through my entire body, was my brother's reaction, or should I say, his lack of reaction.

He didn't seem bothered, or even surprised at all. What freaked me out the most was that he looked me directly in the eye, giving me a sinister smile. I stood there, frozen in shocked silence. I watched him pat the now covered hole with a shovel that he must have kept hidden in the woods.

Seeing the dog collar lying on the ground brought me back to reality. I ran full-force, tackling your uncle. We wrestled for a moment. I stood up, and Mike kicked me hard in the chest, sending me sprawling backwards. It took me a couple of seconds to shake it off, and regain my bearings. Anger was now my # 1 motivation. I charged at him once again, this time pushing him so hard, knocking him backwards. His head hit a large Oak tree. I heard a loud crack. His body twitched several times, and then he stopped moving. My heart was racing a mile a minute, thinking that I had inadvertently killed him. I walked up to the body. I leaned over my brother. I was relieved to see his chest inhaling and exhaling. He was knocked out, but still alive.

My father was continuing his story, when I drove by a commuter parking lot. I could tell that this conversation wasn't ending anytime soon, and I didn't want to waste anymore gas.

I cut off my dad in mid-sentence. "Dad. Dad. Wait a second," I said as I pulled into the lot.

"Are you alright?"

I wanted to tell him about my family reunion which resulted in me being stabbed, but figured that now was not the time.

"Yeah, I'm fine," I lied. "I'm turning off the car. Give me a second. I need to switch from Bluetooth."

He waited until I parked. Turned off the car, and asked, "What happened next?"

16

OK, where was I?"

You said that you knocked him out, but was thankful that he was still breathing."

"Oh, yeah. I went to the covered hole, got down on all fours, and started digging with my hands. I looked over at my brother. He was unconscious, but still breathing. I continued digging frantically. Suddenly, I felt something. I wasn't sure what it was, but I had a good idea. The dog was missing, and I could now see that the area was littered with dog collars. It made me sick to my stomach as I dug. I was both enraged and frightful of what I would find. Panic mode set in.I was able to get a grip around the object in the hole. I almost vomited as I held my favorite pet, Angus', head in my hands. The right side of his skull was bashed in.

Just then, a flashlight shone in his face. It was your grandparents. Now that the light was shining on the area, I noticed hole after hole after hole. All had been filled in. There must have been at least 10, maybe more. I sat there paralyzed with my dogs head in my hands.

The sound of my father's voice snapped me out of it. 'Hey, Richard! Look out!'

"I looked at my parents with tears streaming down my face. I felt a sharp pain, and then a warmth in my shoulder. Mike had regained consciousness, and stabbed me in the shoulder."

My hand automatically went to my shoulder, and began massaging my own stab wound.

"You were stabbed?" I asked incredulously.

"Yes," my dad said matter of factly. He attempted a second time, but your grandfather kicked the knife out of his hand, tackled him, and restrained him until your grandmother went back to the house to phone the police. The police came, and took him away. He was institutionalized until his 18th birthday. He was later moved to a halfway house."

I stopped him there. "Yeah, I read what happened next in the paper."

There was several seconds of silence when my father exclaimed, "Shit! I know where he is. I know where he's going!"

We both said it at the same time: "THE WOODS!"

17

I'm going to get my gun, and find him."

"You can't do that. You're retired."

Never mind that. Where are you?" my father asked.

"Ahh, now you decide to worry about where I am, " I said in a sarcastic tone.

My father had been speaking nonstop for 45 minutes, and only now did it occur to him what I was doing.

"What?" my father asked.

"Nevermind. I just came back from the worst family reunion ever!"

"What's that supposed to mean?"

"I'll tell you all the sordid details once I meet you in the woods behind Grammy and Grampy's house."

"Richard. Stay put!" my father said.

I always hated when he called me by my full name.

"I'm warning you. It's not safe. You don't know how dangerous he can be."

"Oh, I have a general idea," I said.

My father protested again, but it was too late. I hit the red icon on my phone, ending the call.

The rain had just started to come down. All of the windows were fogged up. I started the car, and turned on the defrost.

It was beginning to clear, but not fast enough for me. I grabbed the bloody shirt that I had taken off, and began wiping the inside of the windshield.

I smeared blood, but made a big enough area that I could see out of.

I stared at the neosporin on the passenger seat. "Damn. Once again, that has to wait."

I put the car in drive. The roads were slick, and my tires were worn, not giving me the best traction. My tires screeched on the way out, and I slid to the curb as I pulled out onto the road. I was approximately 25 minutes away from my fathers childhood home. Due to the weather, the roads were clear, allowing me to stay well above the speed limit. I could probably make it in 15 minutes. My father lived only 10 minutes away. If he took his Mazda, he could be there in 5 minutes.

I increased my speed, praying that nothing would jump out at me, such as a dog or deer.

I saw clear road ahead, so I grabbed the neosporin with one hand, as my other hand stayed firmly on the steering wheel. I ripped the package open with my teeth, and twisted the cap off. I rolled up my sleeve, and squeezed it onto my shoulder. I hadn't intended that much to come out, but it gave me a warm, stinging feeling. I figured that meant it was working. Steering with my knee, I used my hand to massage the medication into my wound.

The window began fogging up again. Swearing under my breath, I reached for the bloody shirt, wiping it clear as I can at the moment.

"Remind me to get better wipers once this is all done," I said to no one in particular. I took a sharp left onto High Street. I slammed on the brakes, and skidded to a stop, as I encountered a man walking his dog across the street. I waved, as in 'Sorry for almost killing you'!

All I received in return was his middle finger, and him screaming at the top of his lungs, "SLOW THE FUCK DOWN!"

So much for my attempted apology. I nodded, and continued down the street. I had much bigger problems. I contemplated calling my dad, but was not in the mood for one of his 'Stay put' speeches. The roads were still clear, and I was making great time. It was eerily quiet as I approached the street that led to my grandparents house. The rain was coming down much harder now, and I had near zero visibility through the windshield. I heard a loud THUMP underneath my tire, as my car went up, then down.

"Fucking Potholes!" I exclaimed.

I continued driving, but felt a dragging underneath my rear left tire.

"What the hell is it now?" I muttered.

18

I put on my blinker, and pulled to the curb. I opened the door, and was instantly soaked from the strong winds blowing the rain directly into me. Undeterred, I got out of the car, and began looking underneath to see what I hit. Between the rain, and the absence the streetlights, I wasn't able to see anything. I picked myself off the ground, wiping my pants that were now wet. I opened the car door, grabbed my phone, turned on the flashlight app, and began my search once again. I was about to crouch to the ground to check under the car, when I noticed a large, bulky object lying in the street.

'I don't remember seeing that before', I thought to myself.

My flashlight wasn't much help with the heavy downpour, so I walked closer to this 'thing' in the middle of the road. It wasn't until I got right up over it, and pointed my flashlight at it, that I realized with horror , what it actually was. A body. A human body. At first I was terrified that I was the person that killed him, but then the smell of decaying flesh hit me. An image of the three young men in the back of the Uber flashed through my head. Several crows had been having themselves a picnic until I walked over and scared them away. I bent down closer, plugging my nostrils with my fingers, to get a better look. It hit me full-force. The body was headless, with a trail of blood leading directly to.....................the back of my car.

"Oh Shit!"

19

I hesitantly followed the trail to my rear left tire. I squatted down, extremely fearful, but knowing, what I was going to find that caused the dragging. I worked up enough courage to turn the light facing the wheel. NOTHING!

"Hallelujah!"

I reached underneath to to confirm. That's when I felt something. Whatever it was, it was stuck. I pulled harder. It was really stuck. I went from the squatting position,to lying flat on my stomach, to get a better reach. I looked underneath. I saw a head staring at me. His face was contorted into a scream,much like a mummified Egyptian. One eye socket had been completely cleaned by the crows. The other eyeball was half inserted into the socket, but had been pecked at badly. I jumped up too quickly, hitting my shoulder against the bumper. I bit down on my wrist to avoid a loud scream. Not knowing what to do next, and in semi-shock, I ripped open the door, turned the key, and put the car in reverse. Another loud THUMP meant that I had driven over the corpse once again. I put it in drive, and accelerated my speed.

The head became loose, as I watched it rolling down the road in my rearview mirror.

20

I felt nothing. No horror. No shock. Only numbness. It might have been the extreme fatigue, but nonetheless, my only motivation was to reach the woods before my father. I knew it was useless, but I hit my dad's cell number on the bluetooth. After 3 rings, he started speaking.

"Hi, this is Rich."

I started to speak, just as my father finished his sentence.

"Leave your name and number after the beep."

"Damn!" I exclaimed, hitting the end button on my steering wheel, and taking the next right, getting me closer to the woods.

21

Richard Sr. continued racing down the dark road towards the woods. He used his right hand to steer, as he leaned over to open up the dashboard, looking for a pack of cigarettes. Papers, registration, and old receipts were thrown to the ground as he began his search. He dug a little deeper, and grabbed what felt like a half-empty pack. Just as he began to silently congratulate himself on this personal victory, he noticed a pair of headlights coming directly at him, accompanied by a loud beeping of the horn. He looked up just in time to swerve back into his own lane.

"The doctor is correct. These damn cigarettes are going to kill me someday!"

He fished in his pants pocket for a lighter. This was much easier than searching for the cigarettes. He lit up, inhaled deeply, held it for a second, exhaled, and then let out a dry cough.

"Ahhhh. Much better!"

This calmed him a bit. He began to feel more in control, and less stressed. He took another drag, and turned on the radio. It was already preset to his favorite era, the 60's. Singing along to the Mama's and Papa's about his least favorite day of the week, he stopped when his son's name appeared on full display on the radio, which meant he was trying to call. He hesitated a moment, until he finally came to the conclusion that he would be better off not answering it.

"I'm not going to have anyone talk me out of this."
He ended the call without answering it.

22

By now the adrenaline kicked in, and was exceeding capacity for me. I took a second to collect my thoughts, and realized how fast I was driving. The speedometer read 87mph. I let my foot off the gas. I watched the speedometer drop from 80, to 75, to 60, to 42. I kept it steady at 39 mph. I just passed the sign welcoming me to my father's childhood home of Wolcott, CT. It's a small rural town that is a suburb of the neighboring city of Waterbury. It's much bigger now, but when my father was growing up, it consisted of mainly woods. His joke was that Wolcott only had one main road, with many dead-end roads on the side.

I was really close now. Not a car in sight. My father must have gotten a better headstart than I thought. Either that, or his adrenaline kicked in as well, which most likely eliminated any care or concern for speed limits and stop signs.

My father had grown up on a dead-end road that had been built, and named after his father. He had also built many of the houses, including his family home. I was most impressed with the fact that when asked how he learned to do all of that, my father told me he went to the library, and took books out on the subject. I find it difficult to keep myself from laughing whenever someone cries me the blues that they can't do something because they didn't have enough money for college. My motto has always been: LIFE IS THE BEST SCHOOL!

23

I was now close enough to see the street sign for my father's old neighborhood. My gut was now wrenching with a mixture of fear, excitement, and adrenaline. With so many thought going through my head, I realized that I was going to drive right past the road. I took a hard left turn, without applying the brakes. Just as I turned onto the street, a car backed out of his driveway, without even checking for other cars. I slammed on the brakes, and swerved right, helping me avoid hitting the car. I lost control of my car. It jumped the curb, and drove up onto the neighbor's lawn. Everything was happening so fast, that I took my hand off the steering wheel for only a moment. That moment proved to be disastrous to my car, as it continued farther onto the lawn. My driver's side scraped against a smaller tree before finally smashing into a large oak tree. I sat there stunned. I wasn't hurt, but it took several seconds to regain my senses. The front end was heavily dented, but making it worse was that my driver's side door was bent shut. Unfortunately, my passenger side door was bent shut from a previous accident. Between the cost of fixing the door, and procrastination, I never had that fixed. I was now stuck in my own car. I attempted to open the door. It wouldn't budge, I tried again, pushing my shoulder into it. I screamed out in pain. So much had transpired, that I forgot about being stabbed. I was quickly reminded. I scooted my body over to the passenger side, and began kicking the driver's side door forcefully with both legs. It budged a little. I kicked it again. It opened some more. Just as I was going to give it a third kick, I heard a voice in the distance screaming.

"Hey! Are you alright?"

I peered out the rear window. I saw a man running full speed towards my car. No time to waste. I kicked it a third time. It opened enough where I might be able to squeeze myself out. I dragged my ass back to the driver's seat, grabbed the car door handle from the inside, and began to push. At that precise moment, a man appeared at the door.

"Holy Shit! Are you hurt?"

Still somewhat dazed, It took me a second to answer. Before I could say a word, he took a closer look at me and said, "Wait a minute. Aren't you Richie's kid. I'm not sure if you remember me. I've lived here for 30 years. Your grandfather built my house. It's Enrico."

I looked at him. The Enrico I remember was much skinnier, had way more hair, and had a disturbing looking mustache. Then again, it has been 30 years. "Yes, that's me. Now can you start by helping me get the fuck out of here?"

My father's neighbor stared at me dumbfounded. His entire body shook. This must have snapped him out of it.

"Sorry, man," he said as he grabbed the door handle from the outside, and began to pull. I continued to push from the inside, this time with my hands. I learned the hard way that my shoulder was still extremely fragile. I attempted to squeeze out, but it still wasn't open quite enough. He pulled, I pushed. This time the door swung open enough for me to get out. As I was squeezing my way out, good ol' Enrico tried to help by grabbing my shoulder.

"FUUUUUCK!"

The pain was unbearable. I could imagine windows shattering all through the neighborhood. That didn't happen, but what did happen was that lights in some of the houses turned on, curtains were moved, and curious neighbors began staring out their windows. It was like everyone instantly became Gladys Kravitz, the nosy neighbor on 'BeWitched'. I couldn't blame them. This was probably the most exciting thing to ever happen in this small, secluded town. I looked up at the house, whose yard I was now using as a temporary parking lot. No lights turned on. No curtains being moved. No nosy neighbor looking out the window. I looked in the driveway. I didn't see any cars. Enrico noticed me looking at the house, and knew exactly what I was thinking.

"Don't worry about the Weavers," he said. They're in the Bahama's right now. Lucky bastards!"

"Enrico. Listen to me. I know you're only trying to help, but please stay away from the arm. It's a long story, but I have to go to the woods out back to save my dad from a crazy, maniacal Uncle I just found out I had several hours ago. He introduced himself to me by stabbing me in the shoulder!"

This stopped Enrico in his tracks. The confusion and disbelief, lasted long enough for me to squeeze out without him doing anymore damage to my shoulder. My grandparents house, before they died, was at the very end of the dead-end road. I began to walk that way. I stopped, ran back to the car, and reached in to grab my father's birthday present. Enricio was staring at me like I was some kind of crazy person. At that moment, I wasn't sure if he would be wrong. I put the I-Pod in my back pocket.

"Enrico. Take this, and see if you can get AAA to get this piece of shit out of here," I said as I threw him my car keys. "I'll tell dad you said 'hi'. I'd love to stay and chat, but I have a family reunion to get to that is on par with The Manson Family!"

24

With that, I burst into a sprint up the road, leaving Enrico standing in the yard with his mouth gaping, and my car keys dangling from his right hand.

I reached the top of the road. I was out of breath, and breathing heavily. I stood hunched over, catching my breath. I looked up and saw two cars parked. One was the UBER car, with the keys still dangling in the ignition. The other was my fathers. The drivers side door was still open. I looked inside. There were no keys.

"At least he remembered to turn the car off," I muttered.

I felt something falling out of my back pocket. It was the I-Pod. I threw it into the front seat of my fathers car.

"Happy Birthday, Old Man."

I looked into the woods. I couldn't see anything. I cupped my two hands around my mouth, creating a megaphone effect.

"Dad! Daaaad!" I screamed.

No answer. I walked to the beginning of the trail, and screamed for him once again. Still nothing. I walked deeper into the woods. I couldn't hear anything, but now I noticed some light emanating from deep in the woods. That reminded me to take out my phone to use the flashlight app. I reached into my back pocket, and felt nothing.

"Damn! I hope it's back in the car."

Even though the rain had become a light drizzle, it was still very cloudy. This created a blanket, covering the moon and the stars. That stopped any hope I had for any type of light to guide my way.

"Fuck it!"

I began to run blindly into the woods, chasing the light, which I hoped belonged to my father.

"Dad," I screamed, tripping over sticks, rocks, and overgrown foliage.

I continued running, and screaming. My left foot became entangled in a root. I fell face first, my mouth smashing into a medium sized rock. The pain shot from my mouth, right up through the temple. I wanted to scream every profanity that I have ever heard, but between the shock, numbness, pain, and lack of sleep, all I could do was lay there. I reached into my mouth with my left hand. I felt a jagged tooth in front. My finger had hit a nerve that made me scream in pain, and caused tears to stream down my face. My tooth had broken. Blood began to seep from the left corner of my mouth. I rested for a few seconds, attempting to regain my composure.

25

From a distance I heard, "Put the shovel down, Motherfucker!"

There was no mistaking my dad's signature word.

I stood up, brushed myself off, wiped the blood from the corner of my mouth with my forearm, and began to run toward the voice.

It was pitch black with no flashlight. During the day, this would not be a problem, but the trail had overgrown since the last time I went walking through these woods. My shoulder hurt, my mouth hurt, and I had scraped my knee badly when I fell, causing me to limp. As scared as I was, I still couldn't help but chuckle at the fact that I looked like Jack Torrance stalking Danny at the end of 'The Shining'. The voices were muffled, but they grew louder, as I walked closer to the light. I tripped several more times. I was now so focused on not hurting myself, staring at the ground that I failed to realize that I had walked into a clearing where my dad and uncle now stood. I looked up and was immediately blinded by a beam of light that was now shining directly into my eyes. It was a flashlight. I began to rub my eyes, but saw nothing but flashes. It took several seconds for my eyes to regain focus. Just as I was getting my vision back, I saw my father and uncle standing directly opposite of each other. One held a shovel, the other a gun. I know it sounds crazy, but I found it difficult to recognize one from the other.

"Dad!" I screamed.

Both men acted as if I wasn't even there. The flashlight was thrown to the ground. They just stared at each other intensely, like two heavyweight boxers waiting for the other to throw the first punch. I was becoming aware of my surroundings, and the flashlight on the ground helped by casting a glow. At first I thought I was seeing things, and began rubbing my eyes to clear my vision. Unfortunately, my fears proved correct. I saw a large hole that appeared as if it was freshly dug. To the right of the hole, was a bloodied corpse, minus the head. It seems as if my dear old Uncle had a fascination with decapitation. The stench immediately hit me like a brick wall. My stomach felt queasy, and I wanted to puke. Since I hadn't eaten in the last 8 hours, the dry heaves kicked in. I began to spit up. A loud WHAP snapped me back to reality. It was the sound of the shovel hitting my dad, or was it my uncle, in the larynx. The gun went flying from his hand. Without thinking, I ran to the gun, picked it up, and began pointing it at the two of them.

"Alright. Put the shovel down. Dad, are you ok?" I asked, still not knowing which one was him. The resemblance was eerie. They both dressed and looked exactly alike. It was like watching a horror version of 'The Patty Duke Show'! No one spoke. The person on the ground was clutching his larynx, coughing up blood, and choking. The person holing the shovel, stood silently, staring.

I pointed the gun at the person holding the shovel. Fear mixed with anger.

"I'll only say this once. Put the fucking shovel down now!"

The shovel was dropped.

"Alright. I know this sounds crazy, but which one is my father?"

The person on the ground was still keeled over in pain, and breathing, and choking on blood furiously. I grabbed the flashlight from the ground, surveying the area with one hand, while pointing the gun at the person standing, with the other. I could now see several bodies strewn throughout the area. Not all were human. I saw decapitated cats, dogs, and other assorted animals as well. One was just a skeleton slowly decaying away. This is the same place where my father caught his twin brother many years ago. The urge to puke came again, but a I regained my composure much quicker this time.

I waved the gun from left to right, not knowing which one was my dad, and which was my uncle.

I screamed again, "Which one of you is my fucking dad?"

One was keeled over on the ground, clutching his larynx. Blood seeped through his fingers. I looked at him for some sort of recognition. I know it sounds crazy, but even this close, I couldn't tell. I looked to the one standing. He had now grabbed the shovel again.

I pointed the gun at him once again.

26

"Put the shovel down!" He just stared. The blank
stare made me assume that he was my maniacal
uncle, but then again, this could be due to shock. I
walked, no, more like limped, closer to him, gun still
pointed. I demanded that he put the shovel down. In
an instant he raised the shovel high above his head. I
didn't have time to react. I thought I was dead as the
shovel came crashing down. I cringed, waiting for
the pain to start. I heard a loud crack, but felt
nothing. Someone, or something was hit, but it
wasn't me. I looked behind me. While I was speaking
to the person with the shovel, the other attempted
to ambush him. He paid with his life. The right side
of his head was caved in. Blood, mixed with pieces of
brain, and bones, began flowing onto the ground
profusely. Anger, Sadness, Anxiety, and Confusion
came rushing to the surface. 'Who was killed? Who
was the killer?' I was more confused than ever.
Suddenly a small detail that I didn't think mattered
much at the time, came to mind. I remembered
reading that Uncle Mike had a very distinct tattoo of
a bald eagle on his shoulder. I wanted to check the
dead body for any sign of it. I cautiously kneeled
next to the body, not taking my eye off my
dad/uncle with the shovel. He didn't make any
moves to attack me, but he also didn't say anything
to reassure me that he was my dad.

I continued staring intently at the killer, reaching around with my left hand, tearing at the shirt of the corpse, looking for any sign of a tattoo.

Anger now reigned supreme.

"Why the fuck are you just staring at me?" I asked, more like screaming.

"Why won't you say anything?"

He continued staring, not saying a word. I could now sense a heavy breathing coming from him that was not noticeable before. I shined the light in his eyes. It was then that I noticed blood on his neck and throat as well. Was the silent killer my uncle, or could it be my father, who had difficulty speaking, due to his throat being cut? I cautiously turned away from him, and shined the light on the dead body to my left. Now that it was quiet, I could hear the heavy breathing was really a desperate grasp at breathing. My hand grabbed the collar of the corpse's shirt. I ripped at it. It was soaked in blood, now beginning to dry. Normally, I would be disgusted at this sight, and sick to my stomach, but I ripped at it like it was no big deal. I tore the shirt off with ease, reminiscent of Hulk Hogan in the Glory Days of the WWF.

The body was drenched in blood, sweat, dirt, leaves, and whatever else decided to stick to the body. It was impossible to confirm a tattoo. I rolled the body over, hoping to find some other identifiable marks. When I did that, I noticed a small black object on the ground. I picked it up.

It was a wallet. I flipped it open. To my surprise, it was empty. I searched through the several compartments. Nothing there either. I searched the area with the flashlight. A small glare hit the flashlight beam. I stood up from the crouching position, and proceeded to walk over to pick it up. I continued keeping the gun pointed at the silent killer, not quite trusting who it was, and what he may try. 'Why wasn't he saying anything? Why didn't he make a move? If it was the killer, he would have surely attacked me by now. If it was my father, I would think, and hope, that he would offer some help'. The gasping for breath became an unbearable wheezing. Maybe he was injured much worse than I thought. I made my way through bones, body tissue, pieces of brain, and various pieces of body that were too disgusting to even contemplate what it might be, scattered on the ground. I picked up what appeared to be a license. It WAS a license, but it belonged to Michael A. Zembruski. It was my uncle's. The bastard had the balls to use his real license. Being an UBER driver is self-employment, and there are no background checks. The perfect job for a homicidal maniac! I pointed the flashlight toward the person holding the shovel. A sense of relief washed over me. "Dad? Is that really you?"

27

He dropped the shovel. I was still hesitant, but was no longer afraid of him anymore. I walked over, and put my arm around him. He was bent over, the wheezing had become worse. He began choking. It was if he was attempting to say something, but was unable to formulate any words.

"Come on dad. Let's go home."

He began walking with me as we made our way back to the road. It was still pitch black. Even though the rain had now stopped, it was impossible to see without the strong beam of my father's Mag flashlight.

Between my injured leg, and his difficulty breathing, the 10 minuter hike back to civilization seemed like an eternity.

We finally made it back to the road. The two cars were still there.

"Hey, dad. Do you have the keys?"

He was coughing violently, and it seemed that the bleeding was becoming worse. I knew it was useless to ask again. I saw that the keys for Uncle Mike's car were not touched.

"Come on dad. We will take care of this piece of shit later, " I said sarcastically, knowing how protective of his car he is. He didn't say anything, but gave me a death glare.

"Now, that is definitely the dad I know and love!"

I walked him over to his brother's car, opened the passenger door, and gently helped him in. I sat in the drivers side, started the car, put it in reverse, and stopped.

"Shit! I almost forgot. I'll be right back. How could I forgot the most important thing; your birthday present," I said to my confused passenger. I walked to the car to get the I-Pod.

"What the......?"

It looked like the car had been ransacked. Papers, tissues, and other assorted papers were all over the seat, on the floor, in the back, and underneath the seat.

"How did I not notice this earlier? Where is the I-Pod?" I threw the papers to the side where the birthday present was. It wasn't there. I looked in the back seat. I couldn't see well, but the gift didn't seem to be there either. I didn't have the flashlight, but the street light gave me sufficient light to search. I heard some scuffling coming from the glove box. I leaned into the car to get a better look. Something jumped out, ran up my arm, and out of the car. I screamed at first. I looked outside, shaken up, to see a squirrel happily running in the street with a receipt it picked up in the car. I let out a nervous laugh. It took a few seconds to kick in what happened. Suddenly, I began laughing hysterically. What a way to end the Night From Hell!

28

Now it was back to the search for the I-Pod.

"After everything we have been through tonight, I am determined more than ever to give dad his birthday present!" I said, laughing even more crazily.

I reached into the glove compartment, not finding anything of importance. I pushed all of the junk that accumulated on the passenger seat onto the floor. Still nothing. I leaned in, and began feeling my way on the floor. I felt something.

"Well, it's about damn time! Dad, you're gonna love this."

I lifted myself up, and looked at what I had picked up, using the streetlight as my guide. In my hand was the package containing my dad's state-of-the-art present.

A huge shadow was suddenly cast over me.

"What the hell....?"

I turned around to see my dad staring at me, with the Mag light raised high in the air. Before I had a chance to ask him what he was doing, I saw it. His shirt was torn on his left shoulder, exposing the top of his shoulder, and part of his arm. There it was. A Bald Eagle tattoo.

"Whaaaaa............................" was all I was able to get out, as I saw the flashlight come crashing down. A loud WHAAP, and everything went black!

THE END